ENTER THE PENETRATOR

Johnny Utah had quite a reputation: police killer, narco big shot. A special undercover agent's report on him described him well.

"It is considered here a well-known but unprovable fact that Johnny Utah is the Big Daddy of the narcotics trade in the Detroit area. Since this city is nearly 50 percent black, the blacks who hate narcotics have long considered a vigilante operation to eliminate Utah. Few decent Detroiters would weep if this man ceased to exist."

When Mark Hardin read the report his reaction was swift.

"Waste him!" he said.

Other Books in the Penetrator Series:

No. 14

THE PENETRATOR
MANKILL SPORT

by Lionel Derrick

PINNACLE BOOKS • NEW YORK CITY

THE PENETRATOR: MANKILL SPORT

Copyright © 1976 by Pinnacle Books, Inc.

Special acknowledgments to Chet Cunningham

An original Pinnacle Books edition, published for the first time anywhere.

ISBN: 0-523-00858-9

First printing, May 1976

Cover illustration by Mike Hooks

Printed in the United States of America

PINNACLE BOOKS, INC.
275 Madison Avenue
New York, N.Y. 10016

Dedicated to the real live T.L.K., in Livingston, and to Janie, who put up with a lot from the writer in the early years.

And to Don Shepherd, the Tireless.

—LCD

MANKILL SPORT

PROLOGUE

Mark Hardin was only a man, a very tired one, not the superman a growing army of his devoted followers "knew" he must be. These Penetrator "groupies" counted among their members hundreds of people the Penetrator had helped in over two and a half years of his one-man war against crime, and millions more who had heard of his exploits in newspapers and on television.

Mark didn't plan it that way. He came out of the army broken in body as well as spirit. The army had taken his natural talents as a hunter and marksman and honed him into a magnificent killing machine, but one with a heart and soul and, most important, a mind that was computer-fast in observing, evaluating, restructuring and changing prepared plans to turn a defeat or failure into a remarkable success.

The army had trained him well, then put him into investigation work. Soon he unearthed and exposed to the press a gigantic scandal involving many millions of dollars worth of war goods sold through the Saigon black market. The scandal implicated several high-ranking U.S. military officers, including a general. For not playing the army "game" Mark was beaten up by a half-dozen unscrupulous army thugs, who thought they had killed him. But Mark survived.

Just out of the army hospital and the service, he found a haven with Professor Willard Haskins in his concealed hideaway in the Calico mountains not far from Barstow, California. There Mark rested, recuperated and discovered he was one half Cheyenne Indian. He had not known his parents, who were both killed in a car crash when Mark was young. David Red Eagle, a full-blooded Cheyenne who lived with the professor, soon instilled in Mark the full realization of his heritage and many of the Indian's early skills in warfare, tracking, hunting, stalking and the use of the magical medicine man's regimens of *Sho-tu-ça.*

Later, when the professor's niece was killed by Mafia hit men, Mark took on the task of running those responsible to ground. In the process, he broke up a huge Los Angeles heroin ring and captured $800,000 in Mafia money.

So the pattern was set. Mark Hardin became the Penetrator, his real identity concealed, a one-man crime force with the professor serving as his G-2, working on research and intelligence and keeping an eye out for potential trouble spots around the nation and across the world. David Red

Eagle became Mark's trainer, coach and mentor in all things concerning his physical skills and condition.

Time after time the Penetrator launched into the field to challenge anyone he found taking advantage of his fellow man. Mark swept across the U.S., from Los Angeles to New York, Boston and Washington D.C. He flew to Tokyo, bounced down the dry peninsula of Baja, California, in old Mexico and scattered the bodies of hoodlums and Mafia henchmen in Atlanta, Seattle, Salt Lake City and Las Vegas.

Mark was constantly being sought by the police, by the F.B.I. and various underworld organizations determined to wipe him out. More than one mobster had put a price on Mark's head. The crime syndicates and underworld around the nation soon learned to fear and hate this man who walked so quietly, yet spawned terrible, violent death to criminals. Usually he left a blue flint arrowhead at the scene as his trademark.

The Penetrator won friends in a few law enforcement agencies, such as Dan Griggs in the Justice Department. The original confrontation led to limited cooperation by Griggs—without the knowledge of his superiors, of course.

Mark Hardin worked for the underdog, for the common man or woman caught up in large-sized trouble. It might be a fishing boat captain in New Orleans, a young dancer in

Hollywood or a Kansas farmer who found his cattle mysteriously poisoned.

The Penetrator's vengeance has not been for himself—rather it's been for society, for those who won't or can't strike back for themselves, who must rely on others to fight their battles. Now all across the country, the loan sharks, the shake-down artists, the criminals large and small watch over their shoulders, hoping the man with the blue-flint arrowhead doesn't pay them a call.

Law enforcement officials soon realized that the Penetrator showed up in areas of high criminal activity. Some police welcomed him to their areas in spirit, but officially he was a wanted felon, and was named as being "armed and extremely dangerous," even though he had never fired a single shot at a legitimate, honest law officer.

The police have continued to watch for him. The F.B.I. has a full-time man assigned to find and bring Mark to trial. But the public thinks of him more as a second Robin Hood. They ask, is it against the law to steal from the hardened criminals when most of the money is returned to those innocent persons who had been oppressed and robbed in the first place? Each new foray against crime seems to heighten and strengthen the Penetrator's popularity with the common people, and confuses and irritates another police department.

After the last bloody siege with a private

army of cutthroats in Atlanta, Mark quietly slipped out of the country with Joanna Tabler. He had met this Justice agent in his battle with black extremists in New York*, and the friendship grew. He worked with her in three more campaigns, and the romance blossomed.

Now Mark was gut-tired, exhausted. He needed time to rest and try to put his life together again, to get back on course. He was sure that Joanna Tabler would help him. He wanted two weeks of lying on the sand, soaking up the warm sun and swimming in the clear waters of Acupulco, Mexico.

He let the sun beat into his skin and relaxed.

Mark Hardin was a larger and more powerful man than most people thought at first glance. At six feet, two inches he was heavily muscled and looked like an athlete in training. His general complexion was dark, and he suntanned to a coppery brown when he had a chance. He could move with the supple litheness of a cougar, and his dark eyes and thick black moustache gave his face a smoldering, critical look. When he frowned, a lethal aura seemed to engulf him.

Mark's hair was black and a little shaggy, hiding part of his ears and collar. His best weight was two hundred and five pounds, which he maintained without conscious effort. His accent, if any, was NBC newscast-

*See Penetrator #4, *Hijacking Manhattan.*

5

er, but Easterners and those from the deep South picked up the far-West twang if they listened closely. His enemies usually never had a chance to listen at all.

Mark watched the silver-blonde beside him in the skimpy bikini. He was even getting to know Joanna again. It had been over six months since he had seen her. He turned over to toast the other side and felt the tenseness fading from him. So far everything was perfect. But he had never completed a planned vacation yet. Somehow he had a hunch this one would be no different.

Chapter 1

A LONG UGLY LIFE

Johnny Utah, lean as a picket fence, sucked in his gut as he pressed hard against the cold bricks of an alley just off East Grand Boulevard, waiting for the car to move to the center point of the dark passage. His lips curled in grim pleasure, making his thin face and deep-set brown eyes appear softer than usual. The sedan's headlights were off as ordered. He held his breath in the three A.M. chilly Detroit darkness, knowing his prey would soon get curious and make some move, instead of simply sitting and waiting.

He knew big game: how the hunted reacted to danger. He had stalked and killed every kind of dangerous game, from grizzly bear to water buffalo, from cheetah to boar, tiger to elephant. He had even put his life on the line against a cornered diamondback rattlesnake, armed only with his bare hands—and won. Of course, none of this could compare to hunting up at the lake. This was a kind of hunting right here, he decided, only sometimes it was hard to tell who was the target.

Johnny pulled his attention back to the

7

passenger's side of the two-year-old Chevy. The car had stopped at the mid-point in the slice of darkness between two brick buildings of an old auto manufacturing plant. The passenger-side door came open slowly, and Utah sensed victory as the curly black head of the man he had been waiting for edged over the glass and stared into the misty darkness.

Johnny grinned. He could have taken the man out right then, but he liked to make more of a game of it than that. Utah's conservatively cut black hair blended into the night. He steadied the big Smith and Wesson .44 magnum with its eight-and-three-eighths-inch barrel over his left forearm and brought the red bead front sight squarely on the Detroit policeman's head.

"Back here, Sarge; I got the package for you," Johnny said.

The man's head jerked below the door, then slowly rose.

"Christ, Utah. Don't scare an up-tight nigger that way. I damned near blasted you. You bring it?"

"Right here. Why the hell else I get up at this hour?" Johnny knew he had him then. He could feel the tension ease in the alley, could almost see the expression on the crooked cop's face as he anticipated another fat envelope stuffed with hundred-dollar bills, old ones that couldn't be traced.

Johnny's smile broadened now as the cop

stepped away from the car and walked forward. When the officer was twenty feet away, Johnny fired. The hot load round from the .44 mag sounded like a cannon going off between the echo-chamber brick walls. The slug caught Sargeant Manning on the chin and drove half the bone straight back into his mouth, pushed it past more tissue, then ripped and tore through the policeman's neck bone and heavy muscles, decapitating him. Manning's head, carried backward by the tremendous force of the magnum slug, flopped against his back as his body, which had not yet received the nearly instantaneous nerve responses, remained erect for a fraction of a second. Then his knees buckled and dropped him to a sitting position before his torso fell backward, completely covering his severed head which remained attached to the body only by a few strained muscles and stretched tendons.

The man with the magnum had fired it many times, but never with the hot loads. It took him a tenth of a second to recover from the recoil and whip the sights to where the driver of the undercover cop car should be sitting. Three more shots thundered in the darkness. The Chevy's windshield splattered from the first magnum round, shattering into a million tiny cracks and striations on both sides of the safety glass sandwich. The second .44 rammed through part of the cowling below the wind screen as if it were butter and the third bullet caught glass again. Two of the heavy lead killers bored into Patrolman Korman's chest, spewing blood and tissue around the front seat, making it look like a slaughterhouse bleeding room on Thursday afternoon.

Johnny Utah eased back into the brick entranceway and waited thirty seconds. He heard no sounds, saw no movement from the car. He ran to the driver's side of the Chevy, the big .44 ready. One look through the side window was all he needed. Two more black cops on the take would take no more. Johnny ran lightly for the doorway again, opened it and faded into a warehouse.

Twenty-eight seconds later he emerged on the far side of the block, where he stepped into a waiting Cadillac Eldorado that had its motor running.

The big car had cruised five miles up Woodward avenue, heading for Bloomfield Hills before the first citizen complaint sparked a light on the downtown police switchboard concerning the shots heard near East Grand Boulevard. A prowl car investigated.

The two men in the Cadillac didn't speak. The driver, a small man with absolutely no neck, a wrestler's mangled ears and hair that was showing thin all over the top of his head, glanced at his boss from time to time in the rearview mirror. He had turned down the radio when he saw Johnny coming. Now

10

the gunman stared through heavy brown eyes at the driver.

"Get the news on, Willy."

Each of the eight radio pushbuttons brought only a rush of music. Slowly the driver rotated the knob by hand until he found a news station somewhere in Texas.

"Shit!" Johnny said.

Willy waited a moment, turned one of the local news and music stations down low, then glanced at his boss.

"How'd it go?" Willy asked.

"How did *what* go, stupid? We stayed home all night, remember? We're getting ready for our vacation tomorrow, and I had all those damn forms to fill out for the income tax man, remember? No one went anywhere. We both were home all night, goddammit!"

The silence came and stretched like a plastic shroud. At last the thin man in the rear seat let out a long breath, the last of his anger and tension gone. "It was beautiful, Willy, just beautiful. That's a hell of a piece you got for me. I sure wouldn't trade it for a dozen .45s. But . . ."

Willy glanced in the rearview mirror that was set so he could see his employer. He didn't like taking chances, and he had goofed once already tonight. What he saw told him he could talk.

"But it ain't like the hunting up at the lake, right, Boss?"

Johnny Utah stared at the flickering signs as they passed Nine Mile Road on Woodward and tried to relax in the back seat of the plush car. Damn right it wasn't like hunting at the lake. Nothing in the whole god-dammed world was like the hunting at his Canadian lodge. Nothing anywhere could match it, and he had shot at most of the commercial and private hunting preserves and parks around the globe. But that was sport, recreation. Tonight it was work. A man had to take care of his territory or he wouldn't hold on to it. Especially with the fucking cops. They were the biggest crooks of all. He looked down at the .44 and smiled. If only he could keep it. Why didn't it have a floating barrel like the .45 did, so he could just throw away the barrel and keep the piece with a new unit so the blood-sucking ballistics men couldn't ream him for a snuff? He blinked and looked at the rearview mirror, where he caught the driver's eye.

"No, Willy, nothing is like the lake. I made sure of that when I set it up. Up there it's an absolute gut-wringing challenge, a hunt that can't be described to someone who has never been through it. It can test the guts of any man up to his breaking point, and then continue testing him all the way to his own death—if he isn't careful. You just gotta be there to know."

They rode in silence for a few miles. It gave Willy time to consider his next move.

They were set to go to the lake about noon, and for Johnny Utah that meant he would be driven in this car with Willy behind the wheel. A thousand goddammed miles over roads through the northern U.S. and then those Canada cowtrails. He ground his teeth in impotent frustration, then he relaxed and took the attitude that had kept him in the good graces of Johnny Utah for ten years: he'd relax and do what he was told. That decided he moved from 55 mph to 65 and began his game of hide-and-seek with the highway cops.

Johnny's thoughts had slid back to business. The two-kill would serve notice on the rest of the Detroit cops on the pad that Johnny Utah would take no shit from them. They would get the message loud and clear. They signed on to work with him, and he was the boss. No more of this push for a bigger cut, like he was getting from that Manning cat. Now the whole crew could settle, down, and business could get back to normal.

There wouldn't be much of a flap about the dead cops. Oh, the police would make a big newspaper play about them for a day or two. Then an envelope would arrive at the right office downtown, explaining that both black cops were addicts and pushers and on the take for over five thousand a month. It would tell the captain that it would be much better public relations for the department if the investigation were low key and dead end.

There were no clues, and the two men would be listed as shot by a person or persons unknown.

He hadn't spent ten years building up his organization of lead men, contacts, connections, pad men, and two police captains just to let the whole distributor and pusher network all over Detroit go to hell because some smart-assed black sergeant wanted to put the arm on him for 10 percent. No way!

Johnny settled down in the soft cushions and realized he was hungry. He didn't feel like a drink from the portable bar just in front of him. He was sure Willy had stocked it with ice cubes before they left the house. No, when he got home, he'd have Willy build him one of those big sonofabitching sandwiches he specialized in, get a couple of beers and watch the late movie on TV. Somehow he never could get back to sleep after he'd been out hunting. Johnny drew the .44 magnum and polished it, realizing that as soon as he got home the weapon would go into the gas-fired incinerator and within ten minutes would be only a twisted mass of unrecognizable metal. No way ballistics was going to put the arm on him!

In the tower room of the Stronghold, his hideaway in the blistering desert near Barstow, California, Professor Willard Haskins pushed back in his easy chair so the foot rest popped out automatically. There was a frown on his close-shaven face. He'd just cut off his goatee again, and his chin itched. But the retired University of Southern California professor had a bigger itch to worry about. He picked up the wide yellow paper from a TWX machine and settled down to read it again, this time for details. The law enforcement agency talk (LEA) and its shorthand didn't bother him now that he had figured out most of it. The copy had come in a special envelope from Dan Griggs of the Justice Department only that morning, when David Red Eagle went on his weekly provision and mail run into Barstow. He adjusted his trifocal glasses and read:

USDOJ RESTRICTED MATTER ****
NEED TO KNOW BASIS ONLY. NO
SCRAMBLE CIRCUIT.
FROM: D GRIGGS #101-22USDOJ
TO: UNIFORM CRIME NETWORK
USDOJ ADVISORY/BACKGROUND ALL
LEA US 121253L
SUBJECT: JOHNNY ALTENBARG ALIAS
JOHNNY UTAH. NO OUTSTANDING
WARRANTS. LAST KNOWN OPERATION
DETROIT. WELL ENTRENCHED. OPERATES
UNDER COVER OF A & B TRUCKING.
LEGIT LICENSED TRANSPORT FIRM
COMMON CARRIER, INTERSTATE,
APPROX 200 LINE HAUL TRACTORS.

****SPECIAL NOTE****
SUBJECT KNOWN TRAFFICKER IN
HARD DRUGS. 27 ARRESTS LAST
30 YEARS, 1 (ONE) CONVICTION,
MISDEMEANOR. USES VARIOUS FRONTS
INCLUDING TRUCKING FIRM. IS
INSULATED BY MANY LAYERS
OF COMMAND BETWEEN UTAH AND
STREET OPERATION.

15

ALL LEA DETROIT AREA URGED
CONCENTRATE ON DRUG-TIED ACTS RE
SUBJECT IN FEDERAL PUSH. NOTIFY
SENDER AT ONCE ANY ACTION,
INFORMATION, MOVEMENT.
SUBJECT DESCRIBED: WM AGE 45, HEIGHT
70 INCHES, WEIGHT 145. HAIR BROWN.
EYES GREEN. EXPENSIVE CLOTHES.
ANY CONTACT NOTIFY SENDER SOONEST.
DC
GRIGGS #101-22USDOJ SENDS
EOM

POLICE BUSINESS****
OPEN MESSAGE
FROM DETROIT PD 127413J
TO: D GRIGGS/USDOJ/WASHDC
IMMEDIATE ATTN
RE JOHNNY UTAH INVOLV NARCO
SUBJECT LEFT HERE TWO WEEKS AGO BY
CAR. AFRAID TO FLY. DESTINATION
NORTH AND WEST. QUOTE THE LAKE
UNQUOTE MENTIONED AS DESTINATION.
DEATH TWO DETROIT PD OFFICERS TWO
WEEKS AGO THOUGHT NARCO CONNECTED.

ADDITIONAL BIO MAT REQUESTED:
SUBJECT AVID HUNTER. FREQUENT TRIPS
WORLD WIDE. TROPHY ROOM LINED WITH
"HEADS" HE SHOT. BIGGEST, TOUGHEST
GAME ALIVE. MEMBER RIFLE, PISTOL
CLUBS. EXPERT ON WEAPONS. MASTER
RATED WITH PISTOL. UNMARRIED. WOMEN
NOT IMPORTANT TO SUBJECT. KNOWN TO
BE HETEROSEXUAL. NEVER MARRIED. NO
CLOSE FRIENDS. SECOND IN COMMAND
DETROIT H.J. (BASTARD) DUNCAN. WM
AGE 32. TWO FELONY CONVICTIONS FOR
POSSESSION. SERVED THREE YEARS.
HE TOOK FALL FOR HIGHER UPS.

UTAH KNOWN AS LONER. QUOTE NOBODY
CAN USE A WIFE OR KID TO GET A
HANDLE ON ME UNQUOTE. HAS LONG
LIST SUSPECTED ILLEGAL ACTS BUT
NO CONVICTIONS. CONSTANTLY LOOKING
FOR NEW HUNTING EXPERIENCES,
TOUGHER HUNTS, LIFE/DEATH STRUGGLES

16

WITH ANIMALS. LIVES BLOOMFIELD HILLS,
MICH. ESTATE ENCLOSED SIX-FOOT BRICK
WALL. REGISTERED ALARMS, LICENSED
GUARDS AT GATE AND WALL. GUARDS HIRED
FROM LOCAL LEGIT FIRM.

SUBJECT DELIBERATE AND CLINICALLY
CAREFUL ON TAX LAW. TRUCK FIRM ALWAYS
SHOWS PROFIT. TAXES PAID. NARCO MONEY
LAUNDERED THROUGH TRUCK FIRM. TRUCK
FIRM PROFIT LAST FISCAL OVER TWO MILLION.
OTHER LOCAL TRUCK CONTACTS SAY
IMPOSSIBLE LEGITIMATELY.

CAME HERE TEN YEARS AGO. TWO FELONY
ARRESTS NINE YEARS AGO, NO CONVICTIONS.
HIGHLY INSULATED FROM CRIME SCENE.

WILL ADVISE OF SUBJECT MOVEMENTS
LESLIE DPD SENDS
EOM

Professor Haskins put down the sheets
and rubbed his eyes. He had been following
the criminal history of Johnny Utah for over
a year. The Detroit papers had broadly
hinted that the two shooting deaths of police
officers had been connected with the rampant
Detroit drug scene. They came as close as
they could to implying that Johnny Utah and
his city-wide narco operations were responsible in some way for the deaths. Speculation
was easy to come by. Man-in-the-street inter-
views indicated most blacks believed the
brothers had been on the take from the big
narco wheels, got out of line and paid for
it by having their heads blown off.

The professor pulled out the rest of the file
he had on the Detroit narcotics organization.

There wasn't a lot of material. He began going through it piece by piece.

The Detroit police department had been helpful, but would say little over the phone. That had prompted his wire to Dan Griggs, requesting some official inquiry help. It had produced an in-depth study of the Detroit hoodlum and a strange lack of action by the motor city police. They had a good excuse: Johnny Utah lived in Bloomfield Hills, well outside of their jurisdiction. He was the worry of the Bloomfield township police. Even though Utah's business was in Detroit, he was seldom seen in the city, and almost never at his trucking outfit. As one Detroit cop said: "It's hard to charge a man with something if you never see him in your jurisdiction."

At the bottom of the stack was a summary of the case against Johnny Utah. Below it Mark had added in his customary scrawl, "Waste him!"

The professor looked at two items he had set aside, one a newspaper clipping of the death of the two black policemen in Detroit. It said so much between the lines, the professor wondered if the by-lined author was still alive. He reread the story. Next he looked at a special undercover agent's report he had obtained from his contact man in Detroit. It was neat and concise, less than one page long. The small summary said:

"It is considered here a well-known but

unprovable fact that Johnny Utah is the big daddy of the narcotics trade in the Detroit area. Since this city is nearly 50 percent black, the blacks who hate narcotics have long considered a vigilante operation to eliminate Utah. His fortress, guards and firepower in the Bloomfield Hills estate have discouraged this idea. Few decent Detroiters would weep if this man ceased to exist."

Professor Haskins stared out through the slit windows at the desert, as brown-dry and windblown as ever. He sucked on a shaggy briar he hadn't looked at for over ten years. It was dry, he never smoked anymore, but when he had a decision to make he'd dig out the briar and clamp it between his teeth. The man in Detroit who wrote the final paragraph of the report was black, a man who knew his city, his people. The professor put away the old briar, shuffled all the papers back into one neat stack and pushed them into the file folder, then stretched and went downstairs for his late afternoon tall cool one. A decision would have to be made. Decisions like this, that almost certainly meant the death of someone, still bothered him. He would recommend to the Penetrator that he target in on Johnny Utah and his drug complex in Detroit. That meant the professor would have to make a telephone call. He closed his eyes and tried to relax. For a moment he considered the time zones, then decided to wait for a few hours.

Chapter 2

THE VINE COVERED COTTAGE

"Faster, faster, Uncle Mark!" the four-year-old girl shouted in delight as her hands-and-knees horse bounced across the living room carpet, wavered, then collapsed near the table and rolled to a stop, exhausted.

"Becky, that's enough; you let Uncle Mark rest a minute." The woman talking was Lori Carpenter, tall, solid, twenty pounds overweight and not worrying about it. She had home-frosted dark hair, laughing brown eyes, and a face that was a delight to watch because it changed constantly, totally displaying her emotions, thoughts, wishes.

Mark Hardin rolled over, caught the little girl around the waist and pulled her on his lap. "Look, button, your old horse is plain worn out. *Es verdad?*" Mark kissed her solemnly on the cheek, stood her up and aimed her at her mother.

"Mommy, why can't we keep Uncle Mark? I want him to stay."

Surprise, then joy flashed over Lori's face as she smiled down at her blonde daughter. "Sweetheart, Uncle Mark can stay as long as he likes. He and Aunt Joanna are here on a vacation, but we hope they both can stay a long time."

"Me too, me too!" a three-year-old boy said, running up to Mark, hurtling the last two feet into Mark's lap, totally without fear, knowing his friend would catch him. Mark grabbed the boy and glanced up at Joanna Tabler, who sat quietly near the window, watching the constant rolling of the Pacific Ocean swells. Her head turned at the small boy's demand, and Mark saw again the soft expression on her strikingly beautiful face.

An ex-model, Joanna could flash a dazzling "camera ready" smile anytime, showing off her fine bone structure, wide-set eyes, professional use of makeup and always neat, short platinum-blonde hair. But now, in a few unguarded seconds, her soft private smile was aimed directly at the bubbling, laughing boy. Shining through it came a yearning, a longing, an unmasked wanting that he had seen every time they visited Lance and Lori Carpenter and their two children at their beautiful ocean-view apartment. They hadn't talked about it, not yet, but Mark knew it was coming. Joanna waved at little Chuck, captivated by his miniature grin, his small-sized bravado, and the continual "me-too" demand for everything his big sister wanted or did.

Mark had seen Joanna with that look several times before, and he had tabbed it the "Vine Covered Cottage" warning sign. Joanna reached for Becky, pulled her into her lap, and brushed back the blonde curls.

"Are we going to swim at the beach today?" Joanna asked.

"I will swim if you will swim," Becky said seriously.

"Me too, me too!" Chuck chimed in. He didn't understand why everyone laughed.

Mark watched Joanna with the small girl. Her arms came around Becky for a hug, then she held the child away so she could see her animated face. They were talking softly. Becky laughed, and the glow that came to Joanna's hazel eyes was a treat for Mark. He had never seen her so vibrant, so full of life, with so much purpose.

Becky giggled and touched Joanna's Elizabeth Taylor nose, moved her hand to carefully arched brows, and ran her hand down Joanna's satin cheeks.

"You are pretty," Becky said.

"Well, thank you, Becky," Joanna said, a soft flush of pleasure touching her cheeks. "And I think you're the prettiest little girl I've seen in a long, long time."

"That's because we live down here in Mexico with the foreigners, and they don't have any blondes here. My daddy says it's because of the water."

The adults laughed. Chuck looked around, curious. He jumped up and down in front of Mark to attract attention.

"Horsey, horsey, horsey," he chanted.

Mark turned him over and holding his ankles, stood Chuck on his head. The small boy howled in delight. Joanna and Becky were deep into some girl talk. Mark looked at Lori and lifted his brows. "Is this domestic-kid-bug catching?" he asked.

Lori smiled. "It sure looks that way."

Without looking at them, Joanna boomed into the conversation.

"It certainly is catching, and the shots I've been getting lately don't seem to be helping a bit."

Lori wailed, laughing so hard she almost fell off her chair. She gasped for air, stood and shook her head at Joanna.

"Jo Tabler, you're just awful, you know that?" She giggled. "I think it's time I get started on something to feed you people tonight. You are staying for dinner?"

Chuck, right side up by now ran after his mother as she headed for the kitchen. "Me too!" he shouted.

Becky sat on Joanna's lap trying to get one of Joanna's platinum blonde curls below her ear to curl even more. The woman hugged Becky, then lowered her to the floor and wiped moisture from one blinking eye as the little girl ran into the kitchen.

"How about a walk on the beach?" Mark asked. "As long as we're in Acapulco, let's take advantage of it."

"Shall I change?"

23

"Not into that string bikini," Mark said. "I don't feel like sharing that much of you with anybody today."

She flashed him a secret smile, stood and held out her hand. She needed the touch, the contact. She wanted it, yes, and she needed it. They called to Lori, saying they would be back soon, then went out the door, down the short path to the Pacific and walked in the dry sand, arms around each other, very close.

"Where does it hurt most?" Mark asked.

She glanced up at him, surprise turning to knowing.

"You understand very well just where it hurts, Mark. Two or three places. Mostly just in back of my chest a little to the left of center where that big pump keeps beating away. I've seen the way you look at Chuck and Becky, how you play with them. You couldn't hide all that inside you anymore than I could."

She stopped him, and they kissed lightly, almost reverently. For a moment they didn't feel the sand or the sun, didn't hear the pounding of the surf—there was only the two of them, nothing else in the universe.

She sighed. "Mark, I'm sorry. I told you I wouldn't nag, right? I said no pursuit, no traps, no snares, just love and be loved, and treasure whatever happiness we could grab when time and schedules permit. No rebukes, no demands, no jealousies . . ."

24

She took his arm and they walked again.

"Mark, you know me pretty well. I don't like going back on a promise. But now, well, I think we should talk. I'm really shook. Hey, are you still here?"

He had been watching a sea gull gliding and wheeling in the afternoon breeze. He was there, following exactly what she was saying, and knowing what she was leading up to before she got there. That was because he had been thinking about the same emotions, the same ideas, the same lives. He reached down and kissed her tanned cheek.

"I'm still here; I'm listening."

"Good, because I haven't felt this way since my senior prom in high school, when I knew very well I was going to be proposed to that night. I had been going steady with the boy for the whole school year, and we petted once or twice, and I just *knew* he was going to propose. I was terrified. I didn't know what I was going to say. I didn't want to get married. He wanted to be a farmer—a farmer!"

Mark bent down, picked up a tiny sand dollar shell, about the size of a quarter, washed it off and gave it to her. She kissed his cheek.

"I didn't know what to say when he asked me. I just blurted out some words. I guess I said no. I feel the same way now and I don't know what half of this is I'm saying . . .

"Mark, I'm twenty-eight years old. I'm

25

single. But I'm also a product of the old school, when a woman's worst possible fate was not to marry, and her second worst possible fate was to have her marriage fail. Very high on the no-no list was for a woman to be barren, for her 'not to do her duty' by having at least two children. That is my heritage. It didn't matter that a woman might want to be successful in a business or profession, even contribute to the world or to the well-being of the people. Hell, no. A woman was a female, and that meant she had to get married, stay married, and have a whole flock of kids."

Silent tears came now. She turned and clung to him. He sat down in the warm sand and held her, let the sobs work their way through until she quieted down, now and then taking deep breaths. She snuggled against his chest, then at last looked at him. His dark eyes concentrated on her, only on her. She shivered and leaned back, wiping wetness away from her eyes.

She tried to smile, and he bent and kissed her lips softly, so tenderly that she almost began crying again.

Joanna sighed and looked out at the waves. "Mark, right now I'd give a million dollars to trade places with Lori—to have a nine-to-five husband, a house and two kids, like them!"

"Joanna," Mark said gently. "More times than you know I've thought about the same things. I wish I had a regular job, working regular hours for Coca Cola, like Lance does down here. Then ... then I'd be able to plan and make a home for you—and for a couple of kids. But we've talked about this before ..."

This time she kissed him.

"Darling, I know. I *know*. I promised myself that I'd never break down this way with you. I'd hold it all inside until you left, then I could wail and scream and cry. I promised myself I'd never bother you about some female hormone charging around in my system. Whoever the hell said that women are the same as men just doesn't know! We've got a drive, an urging that men don't even know how to describe, much less understand."

She looked away, took her arms from him and stood silently.

Mark watched her, realizing that anything he said would be wrong. This was Joanna's own argument with herself.

She turned. "Mark, darling, let's go back to our hotel. Right now. Please, Mark, let's go right now."

He saw the hot determination in her eyes, and they turned, walking quickly through the sand to the street, then over to the Del Playa Hotel, where they hurried up to their room. Before Mark had the door locked, Joanna was taking off her blouse and pulling

27

at her shorts. She kicked them aside and came to him.

"Mark, please, right now before something else happens, please love me, right now."

Later they called Lori and told her they would be there for dinner as promised, but only if they could take the family out to dinner the next night. Lori tried to beg off taking the kids—they were absolute maniacs in a restaurant, she said—but at last she agreed.

By the time Mark and Joanna got back to the Carpenters', Lance was home. Lance was sales coordinator for Coke and served as expert trouble shooter, greaser of palms, and general executive for Coke in Mexico. He earned fifty thousand a year and had been on location in Acapulco for two years. He and Lori had known Joanna for years, last when he was assigned to Coke's New York office. He was an ex-basketball player, 31, and in excellent physical condition.

"Hey, understand you lovebirds vanished into the bushes this afternoon," Lance said, grinning.

Lori jabbed him in the ribs. "Clown," she muttered.

Lance laughed and kissed Joanna's cheek. He had his salesman's personality out today. Mark had to even up the horse rides with one for Chuck, then the kids ate dinner early and were scooted off to bed. Joanna took over the bedding down of the kids and returned with the same soft glow Mark had seen that afternoon. The motherhood syndrome.

"Lance, you have the two sweetest kids in the world," Joanna said. "I'll trade you Mark for the pair."

"Now that is one lousy business deal," Lance said. "That washed up 'Nam vet would be nothing but trouble. I'll keep the kids, they can't whip me yet."

"They're starting to eat more," Joanna said. "Wait until they get to be teenagers. They'll eat you right out of your shorts."

"I'll wait, I'll wait."

The dinner was fresh lobster and T-bone steak with all the trimmings. Lori was a great cook. When the food was gone and dishes cleared, they played pinochle until midnight.

An hour later Mark lay in their hotel bed, his arm around Joanna's shoulder. They had been talking about their work and its unholy demands, about marriage and kids.

Suddenly Joanna wanted to cry.

"I'm sorry I'm such a *schlep*, a woodenhead."

He kissed her and held her tighter.

"Look, things just have a way of getting complicated," he said. "All we have to do is try to uncomplicate them. Do you realize that if I did haul you off to a shotgun wedding, you'd be a widow within two days?"

Joanna blinked.

"True. Dan Griggs would track me down and blast me with my own shotgun. He won't hold still for anybody stealing a J-6 agent off his team."

"Mark, you're a nice man. You say good things."

"Joanna, those kids got to me too. The way you held them, how you talked to them, whispered secrets. That Becky is a little jewel. Then the whole home and housewife bit. I think you'd make one hell of a fine mother."

Her tear ducts overflowed; the deluge came again.

"Oh, damn, damn, damn!" she said softly.

Too late he knew he had said exactly the wrong thing. As if in apology his hand moved under the sheets and stroked her breasts. She sniffled, took a deep breath and kissed his cheek. "Mark, I want to think this out and say exactly the right thing, and I never can think right when you're doing that."

He kissed her lips and leaned back, his fingers laced under his head. Mark could see her out of the corner of his eye. She was frowning, making silent words with her lips, fingers stroking her nose. At last she turned toward him.

"Okay, I think I have the words now. Why does it have to be so hard? Okay, I know, everything is hard. But the problem is I'm a woman. I'm that kind of a woman who really needs a man. When you're around, my whole day comes alive; it's new and vibrant and wonderful. I never want to let go of you. I want to get a big padlock and chain you to my apartment. Never let you outside again, just keep you safe and locked up. Then I can be near you and with you and snuggled up against and around you whenever I want. I don't know if they've made up a word to cover all that, if so, I don't know what it is."

He kissed her.

"Now, don't do that; it just gets me confused. Okay, I want you, and I need you, and I understand it can't be that way, maybe never will be able to be that way. So I'll just go on and die every time you go away. Or maybe I'll scream and bite you or lie down in front of your car . . ."

She leaned up and looked at him. "Mark, I'd trade my J-6 rank and my job and everything for an apartment in the East Sixties, or a house in Jersey, or even a ranch in California. I'd settle down in a rush, and you wouldn't even have to marry me . . ." She gasped. "I've never said that to anyone else, ever . . ."

The phone woke Mark at 2:30 A.M. They both had been sleeping. He answered it and listened carefully, nodding. "Yes. I understand. I'll take the first plane out." He hung up the phone and when he looked back at

Joanna, she was sitting up in the bed, the sheet rumpled around her waist, showing off her breasts. He bent and kissed them, then her lips.

"I'm going with you, Mark. I still have three days left on my vacation, too."

Without a word he left the bed and dressed, then threw his clothes into a suitcase. He was done in two minutes and still she sat on the bed.

"I'm going with you, Mark."

He sat on the bed, pulled her toward him and kissed her.

"No, you are not going with me."

She didn't cry, simply sat there watching him. "I knew it would be tonight. I just knew it."

He closed his bag, snapped the lock.

"Can I come to the airport with you?"

He sat beside her shaking his head. She took his hand and placed it on her breast. "Darling, one more time?"

He bent and kissed her, and she drew him back down on the bed.

Afterward she pretended to be sleeping. He knew she wasn't. He bent over her, kissed her cheek, then soundlessly let himself out the door.

Connections were not good from Acapulco. It was the following afternoon before he arrived at the Burbank airport. David Red Eagle met him in the ancient Ford pickup. It was a battered and dented 1948 body and box, almost without paint from numerous desert sandstorms, but underneath it all the chassis and engine were strictly Ford 1976.

"Gigçan-a ha misukaha!" (Welcome home, little brother) David Red Eagle said to his native Cheyenne.

"Uica-iwa stela, ni tunkan, ha." (It is good to be here, honored Grandfather) Mark replied. The ancient ceremonial greeting out of the way, Mark threw his bag in the back of the pickup and climbed into the battered cab. Inside a difference was obvious at once. An eight-channel law enforcement radio sat on a special mount near the dash. As they pulled out of Burbank, Red Eagle switched from the Burbank frequency to that of the California Highway Patrol, to listen for any road problems or traffic tieups.

"Something in Detroit?" Mark asked.

The ancient Cheyenne nodded so slightly that Mark almost missed it.

"The professor must be upset about something to break in on the last three days of my siesta."

Again the nod came, along with a quick glance that Mark knew was a gentle rebuke. One did not question a superior, especially the chief. The professor was Red Eagle's chief and the landowner of their troika.

They rode in silence as the Ford plowed through the heat waves north on California Highway 14 to Lancaster. There, Red Eagle

33

turned right, heading due east along secondary roads, passing Hi Vista before he crossed highway US 395 north and hit the small community of Helendale and then soon was into Barstow. Ten minutes later Red Eagle backed the pickup toward a solid stone wall.

Mark marveled at the way the professor had concealed his retreat in the old borax mine. A strip of blacktop a quarter of a mile long and thirty feet wide blazed a dark scar across the browns and grays of the desert. It had been an air strip for a housing project which never got past the early planning stages. The air strip was an orphan with only one rutted, hazardous old mining road leading to it. At the far end of the strip the sandstone cliff opened in response to a radio signal from the cab of the pickup. A section of the wall was really a double-height garage door camouflaged and built up on the outside to match the rest of the cliff. Inside the garage, Red Eagle pushed the button again and the door swung closed. They left the pickup and walked to a door that led into a 5,000 square foot residence built by the professor ten years ago into the drifts, tunnels and vaulted rooms of the old borax mine. It was so carefully planned into the landscape, and with 90 percent of it below ground, that anyone could walk directly over the hideaway and never see it. Ventilation pipes came up in clusters of growing cacti. Small one-way glass slit windows appeared to be only dark stains in the tower room at the top of the twenty-foot cliff.

The retreat had its own water supply from deep in the bowels of the mine. In another shaft a heat pump furnished heating and cooling from the water temperature differential in a deep water well. For electricity, a compact turbine generator package whirled almost silently in another tunnel, with an outside air intake and discharge. A huge freezer held enough food to feed ten men for six months.

In the tower room, the professor greeted the other two.

"Ah, Mark, you're looking fit. The Mexican sunshine seems to agree with you."

"It does, professor. You mentioned a name: Johnny Utah. Haven't we been watching him?"

"True. I have a complete file for you to read through. I'd guess Red Eagle will want three days to hone you into fighting trim, and you'll need your free time to soak up all the information I have for you about the famous Mr. Utah.

Mark began going through the file with the professor, and two hours later, Red Eagle came back with dinner trays. The professor had a poached egg, a small tossed salad and a cup of weak tea.

Mark looked at his tray and knew it was action time. The main dish was a two-pound, inch-thick venison steak, lightly seared to trap the juices. On the tray sat a quart of raw milk and three inch-wide slices of whole-grain bread. Red Eagle had baked it himself. Mark settled down to eat and the professor turned on the TV set to listen to the news.

"I do wish Red Eagle would kill that venison before he serves it," the professor said. "The sight of that much blood spoils my appetite."

Mark never thought to question Red Eagle or his methods. He sat down and began eating. When the venison was gone, he went back to the file on Johnny Utah. The hoodlum was the brains, the center of a large narcotics operation in Detroit. By cutting off the head of the octopus, the tentacles should wither and die for lack of support, and direction. It must be done. Johnny Utah had to be wasted as soon as possible.

Chapter 3

QUICK JACKPOT-KILL ONE

Mark cleared with the tower by radio at Detroit City airport and settled the Beechcraft Duke down gently on the north-south runway. He had never come in here before. This downtown airport had once been the pride of the city, but now had been bypassed three times for larger and larger and larger airports to serve the bigger planes and then jets. Now private and some business traffic used the airfield, but no big passenger planes.

He taxied to the transient hangar and made arrangements for the Beech to be kept inside. Next Mark rented a car and transferred three suitcases to the locked trunk of the green Granada. As usual, he brought along a duplicate set of "working tools": arms, ammunition, explosives, CO_2 cartridges, a back-up knife and an assortment of handguns and a folding stock rifle. He had enough explosives, detonators, and the new C-5 plastique to put him in jail for 40 years—if they caught him with it.

In the car, Mark slid his Colt Commander into a clip-on holster on his right hip under his sport coat. The long thin stiletto sheath he strapped firmly to his right forearm, where a tightening of his muscle would release the blade and let it fall into his hand. In his left coat pocket he carried a .22 magnum derringer made by Hi-Standard. This little double-action, squeeze-me hideout gun was so compact it could be carried in a front trouser pocket without showing.

Feeling more "dressed" with his tools in place, Mark gunned the classy Granada onto McNichols Road, moving west until he came to Woodward Avenue, where he turned north and headed toward the mile marker crossroads. He passed Seven-Mile, then Eight- and Nine-Mile roads, slid through Royal Oak and Birmingham before he came to the turnoff to the exclusive community of Bloomfield Hills.

Mark was familiar with its snooty nature, high-walled estates and expensive mansions. When he drove past the address he had been given for Johnny Utah, it was about what he expected. A six-foot brick wall completely surrounded all of the place he could see. It looked like a ten-acre plot, with lots of trees screening the house itself, but there was no closed or locked gate, only a light one that could be shut by hand. Tacky.

Mark refined his approach, took out his clipboard with some official-looking forms, adjusted the horn-rimmed glasses, and drove over the blacktop strip that swung behind a scattering of oak and maples. The house was larger than he thought it would be. As soon as he came to a stop in a four-car blacktopped parking area, all neatly striped, a tall, thick-set man stood beside the house's opened front door. His suit was new but not well cut enough to conceal the weapon under his left arm. The big man closed the door and was halfway to the car by the time Mark got out with his thin attaché case and his clipboard.

"Oh, good morning, sir. You must be Mr. . . ." He paused as he consulted a form on his clipboard. "Yes, here it is, Mr. Altenbarg. John R. Altenbarg, 5463 Cherry Drive?"

The man came closer now and Mark saw deep-set eyes, a scar on his cheek and ham hands. Definitely an enforcer type.

"Mr. Altenbarg ain't at home."

"Oh, I see," Mark said. "Well, I'm Joseph Camper from the Oakland County Assessor's office," he flashed an official-looking credential and put it back in his jacket pocket. "Our office wrote to Mr. Altenbarg informing him of our intended visit, sir, and later a telephone contact was made ascertaining that this would be a convenient time for our agent to call. Mr. Altenbarg or one of his associates assured us that this hour, today would be fine. So we have a confirmation. Actually we don't need Mr. Altenbarg's presence here, this is only a routine inspection for reevaluation of his property for the tax rolls. I'm sure you understand."

"Not a word you said," the big man said, staring at Mark a few seconds more. "Just wait right here, I'll be back." He hurried into the main house, and within half a minute was back, trailing another man who was six inches shorter and appeared six times smarter.

"You're the assessor?" the short, sharp-faced man asked as he strode up.

"Oh, goodness no," Mark said with a simper. "I'm Joseph Camper, junior examiner from the assessor's office. I simply take down the information and make a preliminary estimate. The assessor himself never comes out to individual property."

"How extensive an inspection do you make?" the man asked, hands on hips.

"Takes about ten minutes. Oh, nothing to worry about, I assure you. What I look for ordinarily are new structures, improvements, a new pool, additional rooms or a guest house, renovation of the landscaping, anything that dramatically increases the value of the property."

"You'd want to come inside the main house?"

"Oh, yes, of course."

"Sorry, that's out. We absolutely can't permit that; Mr. Altenbarg specifically told us to allow no visitors."

Mark scribbled on his clipboard. "Very

well, I'll take the usual steps. You'll be served with a summons tomorrow, and the following day I'll be back with the Oakland County sheriff and all residents of the property will be evicted for forty-eight hours to enable the assessor's office to make the required inspection. This step is permitted, in fact it is required, by law."

"What? You're off your cork. Who ever heard anything like that before," the thin-faced man shouted. "I could make a phone call to . . . No, I don't know where to contact Mr. Altenbarg right now."

"Very well, just sign here, indicating you refused me entrance, and I'll be back in two days."

The thin man backed away, his lips working. Quickly he made up his mind. "Sure all you want to do is look around for any construction, not more than ten minutes?"

"Oh, well, now, it may take a little longer than that, this is a big place. You may accompany me if you wish, and your friend as well and anyone else here; I really don't mind."

"You won't want all three of us trailing you around," the thin-faced man said, then frowned again, at last shrugged. "Okay, I guess if we follow along, it will be okay. Where do you want to start?"

"Inside the house first, please," Mark said, briskly, efficiently. "Did you know our reports indicate that 83.5 percent of improve-

41

ments are within the structure itself, so we begin there. You'd be surprised how many people rebuild without a permit just so they can save a few dollars on taxes. It's scandalous." Mark caught a grin from the big man aimed at the smaller one.

"Yeah, I bet. Now, come on, let's get this done as quick as we can."

Inside, the house was quietly expensive, not lavish and overdone as he had expected, and Mark had a feeling someone with a delicate touch had decorated here. They moved from room to room, and Mark dutifully made notes on his printed form. The large man left them and five minutes later caught up with them in the basement game room.

When he came in the door he had a .38 in his right hand, the two-inch barrel almost lost in the big fist.

"Hold it, Harry. This guy's a phoney. Got a damn rental car and no county tags. You better take another look at this damn I.D."

Mark dove behind a desk before the big man could get off a shot, and when Mark came up, he had his Colt Commander .45 in his hand. A hot slug slammed through the edge of the desk, narrowly missing Mark's legs. He pushed over and looked around the desk at floor level. Mark saw the gunman crouching near the pool table. Mark's first Hensley and Gibbs 200-grain slug bored a neat hole through the soft upper chest of the man, expanding slightly as it tore through a rib and carried part of the bone into the heart before it slanted off a back rib and ripped out near the spinal column, tearing a two-inch-wide hole. The body slumped to the floor, its motor stopped, the breath making one last gasping *whoosh* at the same time his bowels disgorged.

Fire and move! Mark reacted automatically to his military training and moved to the other end of the heavy oak desk.

"Hey, Arch, you get him?" a voice asked.

Mark lowered his own voice and gave it a little midwest twang trying to remember how the big gunman sounded. He tried it.

"Hell, yes, Harry. First shot. He's done for."

"Sure?"

"Right in the gizzard. Go look."

"You go look, that's what you get paid for."

Mark waited, but the only sounds he heard were cautious steps away from the desk toward the door. Mark stood quickly, the .45 in front of him in a two-handed grip. Harry was three steps from the door, a small caliber automatic in his hand.

"Hold it, Harry, or you're six feet under."

The man paused, looked back over his shoulder and began to shake. "Jesus, you shot Archie?"

"Yeah, and he's deader 'n hell. Drop the pop gun."

It fell to the wooden floor but didn't discharge.

"How many more triggermen you got around here?"

"None, just Phil the gardener. If he heard the shooting, he'll be out the gate and long gone by now."

"Where's the office, the records, the books?"

Slowly Harry turned, his hands in the air. "Come on, you trying to get me killed? Now what do you want? If Johnny ever finds out who you are, you're gonna be in big trouble."

"Johnny Utah will never even know I've been here, Harry. Now show me the records, or do I start using you for target practice?"

Harry was shaking now. "God, no. No! This way, to the second floor. Nothing up there but the truck records, A & B Trucking."

"Sure, Harry, sure."

"Who are you? You from Chicago, trying to move in on us?"

Mark handed him a blue-flint, chipped arrowhead, the kind the Indians really used and almost nobody remembers how to make.

Harry stared at it for a minute, then sweat beaded his forehead. "Jesus Christ ..." He looked up. "The Penetrator?" Harry almost fell down, staggering against the wall to hold himself up. "Look, I don't know nothing about his operation. I'm from the truck company, the assistant manager. He told me to watch his place while he's gone."

"Where did he go?"

"I don't know."

"Where, Harry?" The .45 muzzle pressed painfully hard under the man's chin. He lifted his head as high as he could. Mark's fist pounded into Harry's belly at half power. The man fell to the floor.

"Now, do we understand each other?" Mark rolled Harry over with his toe. "Where did your boss go?"

"He didn't tell me. Something about going hunting."

"Johnny always goes hunting. Where did he go, what was he gunning for?"

"So help me, Penetrator, he didn't tell me. He said I should ask Archie if I needed to know."

Mark picked Harry up, dragging him to his feet.

"The office, Harry, remember? And I want you to lay out everything for me about his drug operation. You don't do it, Harry, and I'm going to start blowing your joints apart. Your elbows, then shoulders, ankles and knees. You understand, Harry? I've got flat-nosed slugs in here; they'll tear you apart."

"My God. Yes, yes, in here." He was shaking so much now, he couldn't unlock the door. Mark took the key and opened the door, pushing it inward, then he jostled the smaller man ahead into the office: steel desk behind two comfortable chairs, two file cabinets, a shelf for books, a TV set and stereo speakers.

"Open up the files," Mark ordered. Harry did. "Now where's the office safe?"

"There isn't . . ." Harry looked at the black hole of the .45 and moved to the picture on the wall. He turned it one way, then the other. A room air conditioner, built into the wall directly below the window, clicked, unlatching. Harry swung the unit out, and Mark saw it was a dummy. Where the guts of the conditioner should have been was a metal box. Harry lifted it out and put it on the table. Inside were records, books. Mark checked them quickly and found they showed the heroin and cocaine buys, where and how much each time, but nothing about names.

Mark went through the files quickly, but it would have taken more time than he could afford. He dumped out half of one drawer of the files, then checked the desk. On top, taped to the desk in the center lay a note. A ball point pen had scratched out the initials T.L.K. on the paper and opposite that was "Op—Livingston. Mont." Mark stared at it, then pulled the note loose and stuffed it in his pocket.

He checked to be sure he had on the second skin gloves. They looked like real skin, felt real and even had built in fingerprints, which was the whole idea. He used different sets of gloves on each job and sometimes changed during an operation to leave various prints to confuse police. The gloves were made of thin, semipermeable plastic and looked real right down to moles, hairs, raised veins and palm creases.

The note was a new element. The initials could be a person, a business, or a code. "Op" could be anything, operator, operation. Livingston had to be a small town in Montana. But what was a city boy like Johnny Utah doing with a note from an out-of-the-way spot like that? There couldn't be much drug traffic there, that was for sure. It wasn't close to the border. Did he have a friend there? But Montana was the Rocky mountains; that could mean hunting. Mark thought he remembered men going to Montana to hunt for antelope.

Mark pushed the note in front of Harry. He stared at it for several seconds, but shook his head. "I don't know what it means. I heard Johnny's driver bitching last night about having to drive a thousand miles over these damn back roads. He mentioned a town that sounded something like Livingston, but I'm not sure.

"Get sure!"

"Okay, he said Livingston, Montana, some place on the way to where they were going."

"Where were they headed?"

Harry shook his head. "I don't know." He waved the arrowhead. "For Christ's sake,

47

don't you think I'd tell you if I knew? I know what you can do; I know what this thing means."

"That's good, Harry, because I'm losing my patience. The name list. Every big operation like this has a name list, a chain of command. Where's the list, Harry?"

Mark took the arrowhead, grabbed Harry's hand and pushed the sharp tip of the flint under Harry's middle fingernail. Harry stared at it a moment and shivered. Mark pushed the flint until it broke through the skin and stabbed an eighth of an inch under the nail.

Harry screamed and almost passed out. He shook his head and looked at the blood under his nail, then back at Mark. "God, don't do that again, Penetrator. List, the damn list ... yeah, he's got something filed under 'charities.' It's a list with the amount of potential gifts. The figure is the expected weekly take in thousands."

"Now you're doing fine, Harry. Just relax." Mark found the file in one of the drawers he hadn't spilled out. It looked about right. None of the names were familiar, but this was not the cream of Detroit society. He spread the list out on the desk, marked it "pushers, dealers and runners," then called Harry over to the chair. Mark had put the arrowhead back in his pocket, deciding not to use one here. From the flap on his right boot he took out a small packet of syringes. Each was sealed in a plastic shield, and each small disposable syringe had a different colored plunger. Mark used the one that would put Harry to sleep for at least an hour.

Harry seemed dazed now, confused about what was going on and obviously shaken by the fingernail stabbing. Mark sat him down at the desk chair, then plunged the small needle into his arm and shot the juice into Harry's flesh before Harry realized what had happened. Two minutes later Harry slumped over, and Mark picked him up and carried him back down to the basement game room and stretched the mobster out where he could see Archie's body.

Back in the upstairs office Mark gathered up the records, name list and a few other files and carried them down to the basement. He stacked the files neatly and left the name list on top.

Next he took out his .45 Commander, quickly stripped it apart and carefully cleaned off any fingerprints on the parts, wiping it down with a cloth. He assembled the weapon, keeping it clean, then took Harry's hand and pressed it around the gun slide, laying down a good set of prints. He left the weapon a foot from Harry's hand with a round in the chamber ready to fire again.

Mark had decided against killing Harry and leaving an arrowhead. He didn't want

49

Johnny Utah alerted yet that the Penetrator was on the hoodlum's trail. The one-kill would give police enough reason to explore the house carefully, and the list of runners and pushers would keep the whole county busy for weeks. In the meantime Harry would have an interesting time trying to prove that he had not killed Archie.

Mark made a quick search of the rest of the house, then the big garage. The car which he knew Johnny usually used was gone and the rest of the place deserted. Mark got back in his rented Granada and drove to the street, then down a mile to a filling station, where he called the Bloomfield Township police.

"Hey, man, I just heard lots of shooting going on out at Johnny Utah's place in Bloomfield Hills, 4563 Cherry Drive. You better get your ass right out there fast, man."

"Yes, who is this please?"

"Oh, I just was driving by and heard it, then I hauled ass out of there so I don't get involved." Mark hung up and grinned.

He sat in his car in the filling station until two police cars buzzed by on a silent call. These cops weren't so dumb that they were going to scare anyone away with a wailing siren.

Mark turned back to the map of Montana he had been studying. The atlas said he should find Livingston at E-5, and that it had 6,883 people. A regular metropolis. He also had to find this T.L.K., who or whatever that might be. Maybe he was a retired hoodlum Johnny was going to stop and see, pay his respects.

Mark doubted that. He kept thinking. Johnny was a hunter. It might be this T.L.K. was a hunting guide, or operated a hunting guide business.

He checked the facts he had found about Utah. The big car, the new Cadillac El Dorado was specially prepared with a bar, TV set and a bed along one side. It was a custom-made job inside, but stock outside. That wouldn't help any. He had spotted repair orders that showed the rig had new brake linings and a tune-up. That could mean a trip . . . but to where? Livingston, Montana, was his only clue, and that seemed like a remote spot for a hoodlum like Johnny Utah. Mark wished he had arrived in Detroit two weeks ago when the guy was at home.

Mark put the car into gear and drove back toward the Detroit City Airport. He'd check out the Beechcraft Duke and stay overnight, then get an early start with the first light. Now Mark knew where he was going! He wondered if Livingston had an airport.

Chapter 4

THE COLD TRAIL BLUES

Mark landed the Beechcraft Duke at Mission Field, elevation 4,656, six miles east of Livingston, Montana, and caught a taxi into town. There was more town there than he had guessed. He asked the taxi driver, a lean man with a jutting jaw and ear-hiding hair if the initials T.L.K. meant anything to him. The driver shook his head.

"Nope, don't ring no bell. We got a Tim Kelly here, but I couldn't swear about the L."

"What does Mr. Kelly do?"

"Night swamper over at the bank, and a lush during the day."

"He a junkie?"

"Naw, no drugs around here. A little pot maybe. You got to go on over to Butte you want any good stuff."

Mark thanked him and got out at the bus depot. Inside he found a telephone book and began looking through the "K" listings. There weren't that many. Tim Kelly wasn't listed. He found three names that had some chances: Thom Kineally, Thelma Lou Kaster, and a Dr. T.L. Klute. He called the first two. Thom didn't answer. Thelma Lou was home.

"Hello, Mrs. Kaster?"

"Yes."

"I'm looking for John Altenbarg. I was told to try this number."

"Who?"

"John Altenbarg, from Detroit."

"Never heard of him. This some kind of a joke?"

"No, I'm trying to find the man, thanks for your help."

He hung up, got a cup of coffee and asked the waitress where he could find Dr. Klute's office.

"Old four-eyes? Doc Klute's place is just around the corner and half a block down. Tell him Bertie says hi."

Mark finished his coffee and went down the street. At the address he saw a sign on the door: "Dr. T.L. Klute, Optometrist." It was possible. He went inside and saw a small man with glasses, thinning hair and wearing a white doctor's coat.

"Dr. Klute?"

"Yes, what can I do for you today?" the optometrist said. Then he smiled. "You new in town?"

"Yes, how could you tell?"

"Know most of the folks around, at least by sight. That's my business." The edges of his mouth crinkled in a silent chuckle.

Mark laid the crumpled note with the initials on it on the glass display counter.

"A friend of mine left me this note, and I'm not exactly sure what it means."

Dr. Klute glanced at it, frowned and looked up at the stranger.

"Well, that could be me. Thomas Lynn Klute. The 'Op' could stand for optometrist, which I am, and this sure is Livingston, Montana. "Who gave you the note?"

"Friend of mine. It's a little game we play. He leaves clues, and I try to find him." Mark gave Dr. Klute his best honest stare but it wasn't a sale.

"Sure. You a detective? With the F.B.I.?"

Mark laughed. "Not really, and I'm not part of the Mafia either. Just trying to find this guy. Maybe you saw him. His name is Johnny Utah." Mark watched the man's face carefully but there was no twinge, no flutter, no recognition. "Damn, I thought maybe he came in here on his way through to get his eyes checked or his glasses fixed."

Mark looked around the shop and saw the posters about contact lenses. That's when he remembered. The backgrounding on Johnny Utah said he wore contact lenses, a vanity thing. Mark extrapolated from the facts and quickly jumped to a new question.

"What about a man named John R. Altenbarg from Detroit . . ."

"Oh, sure; he was in a little over a week ago."

"Good, that's good. Now, could I ask you why he was here?"

"Sure, half the town knows. He came to pick up four sets of the new soft contact lenses." Klute leaned on the counter, took off his glasses and polished them, then put them back on. "Funny about that. I'd never seen him before. Friend of mine in Detroit fit him for the softs but this Altenbarg had to leave before the contacts could be delivered. This optometrist friend of mine told him to stop by here and pick them up. Dr. Green and I were in school together at Pacific University twenty-five years ago."

"So the lenses came here, and he picked them up?" Mark asked.

"Right. I had him try them on and checked his vision. It was a good piece of work, really brought up that right eye of his."

"Good. Now, is he still in town?"

"Oh, no. Not him. He was all fired up to go hunting. I told him we had some of the best antelope hunting in the world not too far from here, but he said he was interested in bigger, smarter, and tougher game. That car of his was something. You ever see it?"

"The blue Caddy with bed, bar and TV set?"

"You've seen it."

"When did he leave?"

"Three of them in the car. Near as I can remember, they pulled out last Tuesday.

Kids congregated around that car so bad it caused a traffic jam."

"He say where he was headed?"

"Just hunting, going north to hunt. I got the idea he was going into Canada for grizzly, but I couldn't swear to it."

"You remember anything about him?"

The optometrist paused for a moment, stared into Mark's eyes professionally, then looked away. "Well, not that I can think of off-hand."

"How long was he here?"

"Oh, about a day. He came on Monday, but the lenses weren't here, so I suggested he stay at the Mountaineer Lodge and stop back Tuesday after the mail came in at ten. He did."

Mark tapped his fingers on the glass. "Nothing else?"

"Well, I told my wife, Janie, about the Caddy, and she came down to take a look, but they'd left by that time."

"Thanks, Dr. Klute. Next time I need my eyes checked, I'll come back."

Mark walked toward the Mountaineer Lodge. It looked new, with all the trimmings. He took a chance and stopped at the three-island service station beside the motel. When Mark showed the manager an I.D. the professor had supplied, proving he was an investigator for Tracers Unlimited, the redhead's interest picked up.

"Looking for some kind of a crook?"

56

"No, just an inheritance thing. We understand that a man was here last week, driving an unusual Cadillac."

"Oh, sure. The one with the bed along one side and the bar, right? We don't see many like that around here. Even had a small gas generator to run the special circuit for a TV set. Wildest thing I ever saw. We did some work on the front end. That driver was a nut about his wheels."

"Were they here long?"

"Overnight. Took off the next morning. I can tell you what day it was, if it would help."

He took down a record book and turned a page. "That was Tuesday morning. Charged him twenty-seven-fifty labor, and twelve-fifteen for parts. And for the long distance call."

"A phone call?"

"Yeah, the guy said he wanted to call for a motel reservation up north. He paid for it."

"Do you know where he called?"

"Damn right, the town, number and charges." He turned the pad so Mark could see. The listing showed: "212-4334. Bonner's Ferry, Idaho. $3.45." Mark memorized the phone number and the town, the way he had been taught long ago in the army intelligence school.

"Thanks a lot; we appreciate your help."

"Sure, can I sell you some gas?"

Mark laughed, peeled a ten-dollar bill from his money clip and handed it to the red-head. The manager pushed it away.

"Hey, no way. We don't charge around here for being helpful to folks."

Mark waved his thanks and walked back to the bus station and the town's taxi stand. He had to wait twenty minutes before the same taxi that had brought him in from the airport arrived.

Mark flew on to Missoula in the Beech and spent the night. The next morning he continued to the small airstrip near Bonner's Ferry, Idaho. He was only 25 miles from the Canadian border. A quick call to the number he had seen on the charge sheet in the Livingston filling station brought a cheerful reply.

"Northmost motel."

Mark asked how to find the place from the airport and ten minutes later had caught a ride into town and walked up to the motel. Inside, a seventeen-year-old girl with coiled blonde braids covering both ears nodded when he asked her about the blue Cadillac.

"Oh, yes, we remember that car very well. They've been here before. Daddy talked with the man, and he got a little drunk and didn't get home for just hours. We all were very cross with him. But when Daddy starts talking about hunting, there is almost no one who can shut him up." She smiled. "And he's a very good father, too. Would you like to talk to him?"

Judson Monroe was a huge man, over six-five and weighing more than two-hundred and fifty pounds. He came from the residence section of the motel, rubbing his eyes.

"Understand you're the hunting expert around here," Mark said.

Clear blue eyes glinted, brows lifted. "Ha! Who's been feeding you nonsense? Half a dozen other guys would challenge that. Anyway there ain't many hunting experts. It's just the guy who is lucky the most times." A massive hand came out and gripped Mark's offered one. "Now there was a guy through here a week ago who *was* an expert. This guy must be loaded, been here before, and he's got more gadgets on that Caddy of his. He's shot about every kind of critter worth taking an aim on, from Africa through Asia and Alaska. Even killed a maverick bull elephant in some game preserve."

"Mr. John Altenbarg?"

The smile turned to a frown. "How the hell you know that?"

"Because I'm trying to catch up with him. We don't know where he and his party are going. The problem is a rabid dog may have bitten one of them when they were still in Detroit. The dog died two days ago. We want to catch up with them and suggest they take the series of anti-rabies shots."

"Goddamn, that stuff can be bad."

"About as bad as anything can get—fatal."

"Then you're in a rush. Well, I'm not sure where they were going. I up and asked him several times but the sonofagun wouldn't tell me. Said it was a private preserve. I figure it's high up on the Fraser river somewhere. I mean all the way to the top into those tributaries that make up the Fraser. I kept harping at him, and he said it was well above Lillooet, maybe all the way up to Williams Lake."

"You lost me," Mark said. "About how far over the border is that?"

The eyes took on a colder tinge. "Say, you don't aim to do this gent no harm now, do you, son?"

Mark showed him the Tracers Unlimited card. "What we're trying to do, Mr. Monroe, is to save his life. If we get to him before the rabies develops, we have a chance. Now it all may be a false alarm. The dog died of rabies, but we're not positive that this dog was the one that bit Johnny or one of his party. We feel we must try because there's a big enough risk involved."

"Okay, that sounds straight enough. You asked how far north? Williams Lake is about two hundred miles north of Vancouver B.C. Up in the tules. Nothing up there but fir and hemlock forests and a bunch of tall mountains and little lakes. From what

Johnny said, there's a good-sized lake on this place where he's going."

"Sounds like rugged country?"

"Ha. You go west anywhere from the Fraser river and you run out of even logging roads damn soon. A big heart-shaped spot in there, a hundred miles each way, where there's not a single road."

"Wish I had a good map of that area," Mark said.

Monroe waved and went through the door. A moment later he came out with a British Columbia road map and opened it to the area over Vancouver. "Got to think big up there. British Columbia is almost eight hundred miles long north to south. That's as big as California."

He traced the Fraser river north to the two towns he had mentioned. Then his hand pointed west.

"Over in there is a wilderness like you've never seen. You could hide a damn army in there and never notice it."

"Can I borrow your map?" Mark asked.

The big man nodded. "Help yourself; I get them by the dozen. And good luck in your search. I guess you don't want to give the police a tip that you're looking for this man."

"Right. We want as little publicity as possible, so we don't have a panic or a big lawsuit. The firm I'm working for is against any kind of publicity. So that rules out the police. I'm sure you've had your share of nuisance lawsuits by guests tripping over their own shins."

"Damn right. Well, are you off?"

Mark told him he had flown in and was looking for a good car. He got the name of the best used car lot in town, which turned out to be the Ford dealer. Mark picked out a two-year-old four-wheel drive Ford Bronco, paid cash for it from his money belt and drove back to the airport. He usually kept five thousand dollars in his money belt in large bills for emergencies. It was part of the hoodlum money he had liberated in previous actions.

At the airport Mark tried to figure out what weapons to take with him. He guessed there would not be a thorough search at the border, but he couldn't afford to be caught with anything too far out of line. At last he settled for a twin to the .45 Commander he had left in Detroit, one box of shells and an extra magazine.

He put them in the bottom of his suitcase of clothes and set it on the car's rear seat. He left the Duke locked in a T-hangar at Bonners Ferry.

The drive to the border was fast, and the Canadian inspector asked only three questions, then Mark was driving into Rykerts and on to Creston, then west. It wasn't a superhighway, in fact the roads were narrow and crooked, but it was a good change of pace from the big freeways. The road meandered across the bottom of British Columbia just above the border until it came to Hope. That was his first target, and there he took Canadian Highway 1 and turned due north up the white-water course of the fabled Fraser river.

Mark still didn't have a clue to where he was going. He just kept pressing north, past Lytton, swinging left off the main road onto Provincial Highway 12, which hugged the river. In Lillooet he stopped and checked at every filling station he came to, asking about the blue Cadillac with a bed. At the third station he found the man who had serviced it. Strange group. Yes, they were heading north. The driver had asked about the road all the way to Hanceville.

"I suggested he take Highway 97 on through to Williams Lake, and then cut over to Hanceville. But the driver snapped at me and said he knew where the roads went. Snippity little guy. Them ain't freeways through there. Just little two-lane jobs, but most of them are paved now."

That night Mark slept in his car down the road from Greg Ranch a hundred yards off the road behind some trees. There were plenty of trees. He had driven into a wilderness of forests. It felt like high country, and logging scars were everywhere. But the forest was being managed well, and here and there, mile-wide swatches of newly planted young trees marched up and over the hills.

On some stretches of road he met a continual procession of huge logging trucks loaded to bursting, the rear double wheels held onto the front of the truck only by a reach beam and the forty-foot lengths of large douglas fir and hemlock logs. Each mile he drove he saw less and less of civilization until at last he felt he had come to the absolute end of the road.

But at Hanceville he found a talkative gas station attendant who remembered the big Caddy with the TV set, bar and air conditioning. It had kept going. No, the driver hadn't said where he was headed with his big-shot passenger who never even got out of the car. But there was only one road up there, and not much chance to get lost. Tatla Lake was eighty miles on up the line.

At the next little settlements, Alexio Creek and Redstone, Mark checked again, but neither place had seen a big blue Caddy.

Mark pushed on to Tatla Lake. About five o'clock, he found a tiny restaurant and filling station and filled both himself and his car. There was a guest home nearby and two other houses. That was the town. Yes, they saw the Caddy, but the man wasn't sure if it went south toward the little village of Twist Lake, or if it headed on west toward Kleena Kleene. Mark didn't know if he should believe the man, so that night he stayed at the guest home, and stretched out on a hand sewn patch work quilt and decided he must be almost there.

Mark was at the top of that primitive zone. Below Twist Lake he could find no more roads, only a massive area of high mountain peaks, blue marked glaciers, lakes and streams. No roads, no houses, no towns. Nothing. He realized the whole land was heavily forested, but on the map there was nothing else showing on an oblong a hundred miles deep and a hundred and fifty miles wide. It was a truly primitive area. What was hot-shot Johnny Utah coming to a place like this for? Only for hunting? He would know the best hunting spots in the world. Was it moose, mountain goat or the old grizzly? A good hunter could find a variety of game out there in that wilderness.

Now it was Mark's job to find Johnny Utah, the hunter.

Chapter 5

ONE BURGLAR, TWO BURGLAR

The next morning Mark gassed up his wheels
and drove down the rough, unpaved road to
Twist Lake. Dozens of times he had to dive
toward the ditch to escape charging mon-
sters with half the forest on their backs.
Macks, Autocars, Kenworths, and Peterbilts,
all careened past, erupting with billowing
boils of dust and their air horns. He made it
to the little community near the lake and discovered it had been a popular fishing spot
for years. Now the loggers had moved into
the area to the north and the one-tavern,
one-store, six-house and ten-fishing-cabin
settlement had been inundated with the two
dozen house trailers and pickup campers the
loggers and lumbermen lived in.

Mark filled his tank at the self-service station and general store and went inside to
pay. The owner checked the pump with field
glasses, then rang it up. Mark also bought a
fishing pole, reel and line and asked about
the best fishing spots. No one else was in the
store and gradually Mark got the sour-faced,
middle-aged proprietor to talk.

"You want me to tell you where to catch

all of our fish out there?" The man asked, honestly peeved. "Hell, no. Go find out for yourself." Mark didn't reply, and the man relented a little. " 'Course, no sense going up to the north shore, too much crap in the water from the logging up there." He watched Mark for a minute, then went back to pricing goods. "Best way to get along up here is to go about your fishing or camping or whatever, and mind your own business."

Mark nodded solemnly and went out to look around. It was a beautiful little lake, maybe half a mile long and that wide, with a carpet of green conifers right down to the edge. Two of the fishing cabins were in use. The dock held a dozen boats with small outboards, and a few rowboats. Most of the travel trailers were hunched together in one area. He could hear a gasoline engine purring, which he guessed powered a generator for the thin, temporary-looking lines that fed juice to the trailers.

The street had been graveled at one time, and all the houses and stores were on a one-block strip. Fifty yards north lay the lake, but from all other angles the heavy rain forest kept growing in, trying to take over the little clearing. The end building was a four-square house, with a small sign outside that said "Board and Room." Mark went up and knocked. The landlady had one room left. Mark took it.

Mrs. Loomis was in her forties and

quickly told him she was a widow for twelve years now, since a snapped choker cable cut her logger husband in half just above the waist. Her black hair was starting to show streaks of gray.

"Many strangers around here?" Mark asked.

"About all we get up here now is strangers. Like that fancy Cadillac. He came back again. When he comes, we always get a new batch of strangers drifting in. I just don't like that man, I don't care what anybody says."

"He the one with the bed, bar and TV set in his car I heard about?" Mark asked.

"That's him, a regular moneybags from the States. Oh, not that you don't have some good folks down there, but us Canadians got our pride too, you know."

Mark felt a tingle of success. This was the first indication that the man he was seeking had grounded here. "What does he do when he stops here?"

"Do? I don't know. Stayed here the night, then all three of them flew out the next morning on the logger chopper. I guess they must be lumber men or something. Wouldn't give you a pinch of salt for the whole crew." She wiped her hands on her apron. "That tall one, I don't trust him. He scares me. I'd just as soon not take their money, but what can I do?"

Mark had lunch there with the other

boarders, then took another walk. He checked out the tavern, had a beer and came back to his room. As he came to his door on the first floor he heard movement inside. He unlocked the door silently and saw a man jumping out the open window. Mark chased the thin figure. He caught him sprinting for the woods. A shoulder tackle brought him down from behind, and when they stopped rolling behind some brush, Mark was sitting on the man's back.

The intruder was short and slender, and when Mark let him roll over, he showed a full beard, small black eyes and a long nose. Mark guessed he was about twenty-five.

"Jeeze, I wasn't trying to steal nothing. I was just looking around. Honest, mister."

"Honest, mister" was the most obvious giveaway line for a liar, as Mark had found out early in his intelligence work with the army. Mark let him sit up and get his wind back. Mark leaned against a fir tree and stared at the man.

"Look, mister, I didn't steal nothing. Search me. I got nothing. You come back too quick. All I got is my own four dollars I hid in my sock."

Mark still didn't speak.

"Well, Christ, say something! Look, my name is Al Stark, and I'm trying like hell to get out of this damned moose-fart place."

"Tell me about this place," Mark said softly.

"Not much to tell. It was dead here before the loggers moved in. Now it's booming. Population tripled, tavern full every night, two knife fights a weekend. Me, I'm trying for enough money to hitchhike to Vancouver."

"Why are you leaving?"

"Why? You kidding? No, you just got here; I guess you'll find out. No jobs except for loggers, no money, nothing. It's the end of the damn world. And there's the 'grabber' to worry about."

"The what?"

Stark looked around, saw no one but lowered his voice. "We call him 'the grabber.' We don't know who or what it is, but two of my friends have vanished up here, disappeared into thin air. No lie. I was drinking in the Timber Bar with my little buddy Joey, and when I came to the next morning, he was gone. Nobody knew where he was, nobody even remembered seeing him that night. But I sure do. He was there, and now he's gone—vanished."

"He probably hitchhiked out of here."

"In the middle of the night? No way. Joey was so afraid, he wouldn't go no place without me. We came up from California together, hitched the whole way. He was a nice little guy, but chicken. He and me talked about this other guy who vanished. The one before Joey. Somebody said it might be wolves. You know how they work in a pack? They can kill a moose, find one in deep snow

70

and circle it, dart in, nip, dart out, wear the beast out, then when it goes down they get its throat. A man, half-drunk maybe, wouldn't be no match for fifteen, maybe twenty timber wolves in a pack."

"You're drunk, Stark. Making up fairy tales."

"No lie. Hey, you ask anybody. They'll tell you if they're honest. I've heard reports from other places up here, too. Guys just show up missing."

"Sure they do, and Stark, you're an Eagle Scout. What would you do if you had ten bucks?"

"Probably stay drunk for three, four days. But now if I had fifty . . . yeah, with fifty I could buy my way to Vancouver and get a good job."

Mark caught Stark's hand and turned it over. It was smooth, soft. No callouses on fingers or palm.

"A job? You haven't worked in a year."

"So I could turn over a new leaf, what?"

"What yourself. You want to earn a few dollars?"

"True."

"You know that fancy Cadillac that came in about a week ago?"

"Right, mate."

"Where did it go, and where are the three men?"

"That's part of the mystery. No one knows, not much talk about it, but we all

71

wonder. They took off in a chopper somewhere. The logging people use it, and it
swooped in here and picked up these three
gents and left. Flew out due north, if it's
any help."

"The car?"

"Oh, that's a dandy. You know it has a
bed in it and a TV set?"

"Where is it?"

"They put it in a garage and locked it up
tight. Every time they come, they use that
garage, and pay well for it."

Mark's computer was working full speed.
So Johnny Utah had come here, double confirmation, and then left by chopper. Where
to? Mark peeled two twenties off his money
clip and gave them to Stark—then took them
back and gave him a Canadian five-dollar
bill.

"Hey, what . . ."

"I owe you thirty-five; the five's on account. You show up with forty dollars and
somebody will get suspicious. Right?" Now
keep your ears open, and your eyes. Anybody
around here who doesn't seem to work but
has plenty of cash?"

Stark thought a moment. "One guy they
call Big Jack. Don't know what he does, but
he's usually around—except when he goes
fishing. Never seen him bring home any fish,
though. He hangs out at the Timber Bar.
He's probably there now."

"I'm going to prowl around a little. You

see what you can find out and let me know. I'm interested in your uh, 'grabber.' I'll pay for anything you come up with. Now relax."

They stood up, and Mark's right fist swung into Stark's gut. He pulled it so he barely hit the kid, then pushed him down with his other hand.

"That's so if anybody is watching, it won't look like we're friends."

Stark moaned and curled up on the ground. Mark watched him for a moment, decided he was faking it and walked back to his room, closed the door and window, locking both, then went to the general store.

He spent the rest of the afternoon asking questions, looking at the lake and getting in the way. About five o'clock he went into the Timber Bar and spotted a new man. It had to be Big Jack. He was about six-two, well built but showing flab. The bartender was short, fat, with the red cheeks of a boozer and had only a fringe of gray hair around his bald pate. He drew a tap beer when Mark held up one finger, and slid it across the polished bar.

"Catch any fish yet?"

"Haven't wet a fly. I'm onto something else that I can't understand."

"What's that?"

"Well it sounds double-dumb. My crazy sister-in-law said her brother came up here camping and fishing last month and just vanished. Never came home, no phone call, no letter, nothing. His car disappeared and him with it. Nobody's seen him, and the authorities are no help. She thinks he's dead. I told her he just took off for Calgary or somewhere. I can't find hide nor hair of the joker."

Big Jack slid along the bar and joined the group.

"This guy have a name?"

"Sure, Anderson, Andy Anderson."

"Middle-sized guy, maybe five-ten or eleven?"

"Could be."

"We had an Anderson here for a while, then he went to Alaska to work on the pipeline. Said he could make five thousand a month up there."

"Couldn't be the same guy. This Anderson is a dentist who makes a hundred thousand a year."

"I say he was the same guy. He was tired of filling teeth."

Mark backed up a step. "You say any damned thing you want to."

Big Jack grabbed Mark's shirt front and twisted, pulling Mark toward him. Mark played the game and held back, feigning fear.

"Look, wise mouth, we don't need you around here. We don't like smart-assed outsiders, hear? Why don't you get in your car and go fish somewhere else."

"Why don't you . . ." Mark toned down his

angry reply, evidently capitulating, playing the role ". . . let go of my shirt, so I can?"

Slowly the hand relaxed. When it let go of the cloth, it came across Mark's cheek in a vicious full-hand slap that spun Mark half around. Mark held his anger, controlled the first touch of fury with the knowledge that he had something, a lead, the best lead he had run into yet. He turned and walked out the tavern door, ignoring the laughter behind him.

On his way back to the boarding house he heard a call from a patch of dense woods next to the graveled street. Mark saw Al Stark motioning to him. A moment later he found Al behind a big fir tree.

"Got something for you. I see you met Big Jack. Hell of a nice guy, ain't he? What I just found out is that Big Jack always seems to be around the day somebody disappears, and then he's gone the next day. Like they vanish at night, and Big Jack is gone at the same time. Maybe Big Jack is the grabber?"

"Might be. Where does he stay?"

"At your boarding house, second floor back, room number six."

"Anything to tie Big Jack with the Cadillac man?"

"Not that I know of."

Mark turned to leave.

"Hey, man, ain't that worth something on my account?"

Mark gave him a twenty, figuring he had

all he would get from Stark, and walked to the street. He went directly to his room, took out his .45 and checked it. Then he changed his mind and pushed it back. That was no way to play the part, to be a Milquetoast. What he had to do now was get into Jack's room and check it out. There might be a tie-in. If so, what was it and with whom? He went up the stairs quietly, picked the simple lock on the door to number six and was inside.

The room was much like his own, only more lived in. Mark knew where to look, checking for letters, notes, messages. He found nothing. Then he up-ended a chair and saw a small address book taped to the bottom. He leafed through it and noticed some names underlined in red. One of them was Johnny Utah. Mark knew now, the vanishing men and the presence of Johnny Utah must have some connection. It had to. He had no hard evidence, but it was worth a try. He put the book back and had it taped in place when he heard a noise outside the door. It jolted open and Big Jack stood there, surprise on his face, and an ugly .38 in his hand. It was pointed straight at Mark's heart.

Chapter 6

KILL DAY AT THE OFFICE

Queens, New York City—Toombs Antonucci leaned back in the leather swivel rocker executive chair behind his massive cherrywood desk and lit an honest-to-God Havana cigar. How he obtained them was his secret. He put the sterling silver desk lighter back in place and waved at the Turk who had just come in. Toombs wasn't in the mood for bad news, and he knew the Turk wasn't happy. So what the hell, he would sit and enjoy life for another minute.

His office, yeah, he enjoyed his office. Ten thousand bucks he had paid to have it redecorated and stylishly antiquated so it has the turn of the century look, but with all the modern conveniences.

Antonucci sighed. He knew he was putting on weight and promised himself he'd get back on his exercise routine next week. He blew a perfect smoke ring and watched it drift toward the ceiling. Toombs was a medium-sized man by today's physical standards: five-eleven. But at fifty years he still had all of his hair and teeth and a vise-grip on this end of Queens.

Toombs wasn't associated with any of the big three organizations; he had his own corner carved out and protected, and nobody gave him any shit. That was the important part. He had the respect of his family, of his associates and of the stupid general public which flocked to his three Antonucci restaurants. The prices were deliberately kept low and the entertainment the best he could buy. He never made a dime on his eateries. Paid good wages. The restaurants were his hobby, his cover, his ticket to respectability. Since when did a man have to make money on his hobby?

Hell, he was set up perfectly. He never pushed any of the big three, and they let him alone. Usually. So he wasn't rich, he was making half a million clear a year that Uncle Sam didn't know about. He paid his taxes regularly on the pittance he cleared in the restaurants. Fair was fair.

Toombs, who won his nickname in the early days when he spent half his time in the old Tombs jail, turned slowly now, blew a smoke ring at the Turk and belched.

"What the hell you want?"

"It's Schmidt. He's gonna take some heavy persuading," the Turk said. The man stood rangy and thin, with sunken eyes, a shadow beard showing although it was only ten thirty in the morning. The Turk's nose was too long and sharply hooked; black hair shrouded his ears. High cheekbones accented his skull-like look. Toombs had never liked the Turk, but he was the best man in the business when it came to persuasion.

"He needs convincing, convince him."

"You said no heavy work unless you were there."

"Yeah, dammit, all right. Where the hell you got him?"

"The ice house."

A half hour later they were at the Queens Coal and Ice Co. lot. It was a huge complex, now half-outmoded, but still doing a fair business in both ice and coal. The room was at the back of the building, near the railroad tracks, and had been used at one time for holding hundred-pound blocks of ice. It was well insulated and soundproof. Now it was a catch-all storage area, since the ice business had "melted" away to half of its former volume.

Herman R. Schmidt sat on a three-legged stool in the bare room. A single shaded bulb burned over him, casting a circle of light only on the stool. Toombs sat in a chair well out of the glow. He had been extremely careful of this sort of activity during the past ten years. Only three times had he risked the ire of the law enforcement people, when they found a body of a former associate or enemy. It took brains to run a tight operation right under the cops' noses—brains and old-fashioned guts. But you had to know when to stop, when to obey the law, when to pay your taxes and when to pat the local ward healer on his cheating head.

He'd begun with a small restaurant almost thirty years ago and he had made a living. Gradually he got into numbers and off-track betting. He didn't monkey around with narcotics or girls. It made a neat, clean and profitable operation, but not one profitable enough for the big three to move in and squeeze him out. It was his success formula and it had worked for the past twenty-five years. Toombs sighed and looked at the Turk.

It happened so fast Schmidt didn't see it coming. He was told to stand, then the Turk slapped his face one way and then the other. While Schmidt registered surprise, the Turk's left fist slammed hard into his belly. Schmidt grunted and bent over just in time to take the Turk's bony knee in his face. The force of the knee kick toppled Schmidt on his back and broke three teeth.

Schmidt lay where he had fallen on the cold cement floor.

"Now, Mr. Schmidt, let's get our facts straight," the Turk said. "You work for Archie North, correct?"

The man on the floor didn't move. A bucket of ice water sloshed onto Schmidt's chest and face, and he screamed, sat up blinking, swearing in the cone of harsh light.

"You work for Archie North, right?"

"Hell, no."

The Turk kicked Schmidt from the back,

just above the hip bone and below his rib cage, smashing his toe into the man's sensitive kidney. Schmidt choked down a scream, his body jerking with paroxysms of pain as his legs drew up to his chest to dampen the agony.

"You work for Archie North?"

"Yes," blubbered Schmidt.

"Now we're getting somewhere. It won't hurt so much now. Just keep talking. Why were you crowding in on our territory?"

"Not crowding in, honest."

The Turk's toe slammed his vulnerable kidney again, and Schmidt couldn't stop the scream.

When his cries bubbled down, and he could talk again, Schmidt explained haltingly: "Look. I sent two guys to the wrong street. So help me, I got mixed up. I been working alongside you guys five years. No problems. I wasn't trying to expand."

Turk loomed over him, a soldering iron in hand. "Did you say it just the way Johnson told you to? Just the way you rehearsed it, in case we caught you trying to muscle in on our territory?"

"No! Johnson didn't tell me to do anything, except to stay on my side of the fence."

Schmidt screamed again when the dripping solder fell on his shirt, burned through and cooled as it pitted his flesh. He pawed at the hot drops. The Turk used his knife and slit the man's shirt up the back, jerking it off his shoulders, ripping off buttons. The molten solder sizzled this time as it fell on the warm skin of Schmidt's chest.

"Jesus Christ, I can't take no more of this!" Schmidt screamed.

"Shut up, Herman," the Turk said.

Schmidt crawled toward him, hands clawed. The Turk kicked him in the face, slamming him backward, knocking out a front tooth, cracking Schmidt's jaw. He rolled over, moaning.

"Johnson told you to try us, right? Told you to work a few numbers on our side of the line, and when you got away with it, move in and take over the whole block, then the street, right? And Johnson would pay you a hundred a day for every street you stole from us, right?"

Schmidt shook his head. "No," he said, spitting out a broken tooth.

The Turk moved closer with the soldering iron. It was the kind plumbers used to have, a big one, an inch in diameter, with a head three-fourths of an inch square, tapered to a point. It could get red hot, hot enough to burn through a one-inch board.

The man with the skull-face knelt, put his knee on Schmidt's chest, and waved the red-hot iron in his face. "Tell us true, Schmidt, or it's all over for you. *Capish?* Tell us exactly the deal Johnson made with you."

"Dammit, no deal, you cocksucker!" Schmidt bellowed.

The Turk lowered the hot iron, let it touch Schmidt's white skin and drew a quarter-inch deep furrow down his belly. The man hissed inarticulately and passed out.

The bucket of ice water brought Schmidt back to the conscious world, screaming, the words not making sense, the raw desperate pain flashing through, the unbearable agony blubbering out.

In the shadows Toombs Antonucci watched with only half an eye and no ear whatsoever. This didn't happen often in his operation. He could remember only three times in the last ten years he had called on the special services of the Turk. He lived in Chicago and was available on a consulting basis anywhere in the country. Instead of watching, Toombs thought about his long struggle.

The restaurant had made money at first, only a little, but it had been a living and he had been happy cooking and working hard. Then the betting began, and soon he was making more money from the book than the food. His old friend, now in Detroit, Johnny Utah, had stopped by one day to eat and counseled Toombs on the best way to set up and run a book. Then he was really in business, with just enough cops on the pad, just enough word out, and taking no action too big, nothing that would wipe him out.

The numbers operation came in next, and soon it all grew and grew.

His wife knew, and eventually his son discovered, just where the money came from. But his two daughters still thought he was a whiz at the restaurant business. Thank God they weren't accountants. His son decided he'd go to law school instead of coming into the firm. He was there now, with one more year to go. Then Antonucci would have a real mouthpiece when he needed one.

Toombs looked up and saw more ice water splashed on the man. This had not been a simple mistake for Schmidt. He had been warned twice to stay on his side of the line. The last time one of Johnson's men had been there and pistol whipped the messenger. That was going too far. An object lesson with Schmidt had to be made quickly so no other street men would prowl outside of their territory.

It was just a part of the business. Toombs didn't particularly enjoy it, nor did he dislike it. It was like balancing the books; it had to be done, so what's to love or hate?

Toombs saw the square end of the soldering iron press downward until the inch-long point had vanished into Schmidt's fat gut. The scream was that of a wounded, helpless animal, and he passed out again. More ice water.

When Schmidt came back this time, he

held up one hand painfully. There were burn marks on his palm.

"No more. No more. I made the try. I'll come over. Give you what you want about Johnson, tell you where he's weak."

The Turk nodded, and Antonucci left his chair. The Turk laid the soldering iron on Schmidt's chest. They watched it burn, sinking into the flesh from its own weight as Schmidt's scream died in a horrible gargle.

Then both men shot Schmidt in the head. The Turk understood. It was a kind of mutual distrust. Both had been in on the kill, both were liable, responsible, and neither would talk.

It took the Turk eight hours to finish the job. He nailed the forms together from two-by-eights, poured three inches of concrete and let it set for two hours. Then he laid Schmidt in, face up, and poured the rest of the form full, covering the body with the wet, just-mixed concrete. It was the only safe way to do the job, and the Turk did it all himself. In the trade it was known as a Jimmy Hoffa overcoat.

Two days later the cured cement block went into a landfill at the edge of the bay, and a bulldozer buried it in twenty feet of water which was filled in with trash and rich new fill earth.

Toombs watched the burial from his Lincoln Continental Mark IV, through binoculars. No mistake, Herman R. Schmidt had vanished, pulled a Jimmy Hoffa. Now, back to the more pleasant business at hand. He drove the Mark IV himself, wheeling it through the early evening traffic back to his end of town. He didn't drive to the restaurant, stopping instead at a fashionable townhouse highrise. Toombs parked in a special V.I.P. slot in the parking garage and nodded when the door man saluted, then took the elevator to apartment 12-F. His knock on the door brought a scurry inside, inspection through a peephole and a hasty unlatching of the door.

The man on the inside was heavyset, reliable. He had been given a free hand, his only responsibility was to keep the girl in the apartment. He had handcuffed her to the bed.

"Quiet?"

"Yeah, Mr. Antonucci. Quiet. She's been crying."

"Do her good." Toombs pulled off his hat and the light top coat and dropped them on a chair. In the bedroom he found her lying on the bed. Her name was Marci Logan, twenty-two years old, a tiny girl with big jugs and a fine figure and long blonde hair to go along with a pixie-cute face. Her only problem was she had a mind of her own. Blue eyes glared at him. She sat up, jerked at the handcuffs and winced.

"You ready to talk sense now, Marci?"

"A killer? I talk sense to a killer? I

thought you were just a sugar daddy who wanted a good time for the rent. I won't talk with a killer."

"I told you, the paper told you, he was hit by a car on the expressway. You want me to give you a signed statement in blood?"

"Shove it, buster. I want out, free and clear, and fifty thousand in cash. That's all. I've seen you pay off twice that much."

"Not for blackmail, little girl."

"Look, he was up here, and we talked. Then you came, got mad and had a fight, and some more goons came. The next morning the paper says this union guy shows up on the freeway dead. Hit and run they say. You give me what I want, and I forget what I saw. Fair is fair." She watched him, saw no progress and switched her tactics. "Come on, Toomy, baby, you know I won't never say nothing. It spooked me, but I need some goddammed money of my own."

"That's a lot of walking-around dough." He went to the phone and dialed, then spoke quickly. "Brenda? I'll be at the apartment number if anything urgent comes up. Thanks."

When he put down the phone, he sat watching her. It had been one of those unfortunate things. Joey should never have come here. It got out of hand. But it had happened and now he had one little witness too many. His boys were solid, all reliable, no worry there—but this small blonde bitch was not.

87

"Look, Toomy, baby, why not just cancel all this? We can go on like before. I won't say a word, there hasn't been any cops nosing around or anything. We're in the clear! We can get back to enjoying life like we used to, back before." The blouse had fallen open now and dropped off one shoulder, exposing her left breast.

He shook his head. "You're a risk, too damn big a risk. You know too much about my whole operation. I never should have let that happen." He shook his head, amazed. "It's surprising what a pretty young face and a good set of tits like yours can do to a guy my age. I never shoulda let it happen."

He went back to the living room, then to the kitchen and opened a can of beer from the refrigerator. The man behind him stood at the door, arms crossed on his wide chest, in protective command. Antonucci thought about the girl as he drank the beer. There simply seemed no other way.

The phone rang before the beer was gone.

Two long strides and the muscle at the door picked up the handset and answered. He listened for a moment, then held out the phone to Toombs.

"Yes, Toombs Antonucci here. Long distance? Right. Who? Johnny Utah. Christ, I ain't heard from you in a year. What the hell's happening?"

"Got a little hunting trip you can't say no to, Toombs. It's set up right and no problems. Remember when I stopped by and we talked about the ideal type of hunting? Well it's all in place and working. No shit! Want you to come up as my guest. Fly into Vancouver, British Columbia, up above Seattle, and I'll have a car waiting for you."

"Hunting? I don't know, Johnny. I've got a few problems right now. Personnel problems."

"Hey, you forgetting the *type* of hunting we were talking about, Toombs? The biggest game!"

Suddenly Toombs face cracked into a grin. "Oh, yeah, now I remember. You really put that together?"

"Working and rolling. Been open two months now. It's wild, Toombs. Wild! Tests a man right down to his raw guts!"

Toombs Antonucci was thinking. He made up his mind quickly. "Can I come up right away, fly in tomorrow? I've got somebody I want to bring with me."

"Hell yes! Come on. That guest, is it part of that personnel problem you talked about?"

Toombs laughed. "You're quick, Johnny, quick as ever."

"Yeah, that's the problem, and I'll bring her with me."

There was a pause.

"Her? ... Yeah, hell, why not? Give us a little variety. See you as soon as you get up here." He gave Toombs a phone number to call in Vancouver airport when he arrived, and they hung up.

Toombs looked at the thickset man at the door.

"First thing tomorrow morning I'll take your problem off your hands. I think I've found the ideal solution for her."

Chapter 7

A BASH ON THE HEAD

Mark Hardin stared at the .38's black muzzle, then up at the angry face of Big Jack.

"What the hell are *you* doing prowling my room?"

"Just looking around, why?" As he said it, Mark feinted one way, saw the gun swing with him, feinted the other way, then lunged in the original direction and saw that the gun hand wasn't tracking him. The movement brought him closer to the big man and before Jack could correct his arm swing, Mark had chopped the .38 from his hand and elbowed him in the face. The Penetrator then took the steps four at a time, barged through the front door and into the dusty street to his car. He had it started and moving before Big Jack had recovered and grabbed his .38. Mark was in second gear by then and accelerating with the gas pedal jammed to the floorboard. No shots were fired.

Mark made a dust storm getting out of the village and on the way began to work out his plan. He'd been considering it ever since he'd concluded there must be a connection between the missing men, Big Jack and the helicopter. The fact that Johnny Utah had been taken away in the chopper was a strong tie. What was this world-class hunter *doing* up here in the wilderness?

Mark drove carefully for three miles, then found what he wanted, a logging road that led back off the main track. He followed it a quarter of a mile and put the Bronco behind a full screen of young firs. As the dust settled he tried to figure out exactly what he should do next.

His general plan was solid. This was the end of his hot trail. He had to find out more about the connection between Big Jack and Johnny Utah. But he had blown his cover in the village. He couldn't even walk in now and talk to them. So he had to go in some other way.

Mark thought about what he had so far; it wasn't much, and no D.A. in the world would ask for an indictment. The chopper taking Johnny Utah and party away to some undisclosed point; the report of at least three men missing, being "grabbed"; the lumber helicopter making occasional visits to the little lake community. Then he had to consider the reliability of the report by Stark about the missing men. He had been scared enough. Stark would have nothing to gain by his stories if they weren't true.

The final straw of fact came booming down to do the job. He had nothing else. The trail dead-ended here. There was no new direction, no new clues. Everything hinged on the Twist Lake connection. He had to check that out in depth.

So he needed a disguise. No time to drive back to civilization and work up one. He had to go with what he had. For a moment Mark turned the rearview mirror so he could see himself. The idea began to come. Yes. He would go back as a bum, a drifter, a down-and-outer. Exactly like the men who were being grabbed. Maybe he could play bait, and they would take him.

Mark looked around. He'd need a few items. But all of his gear, clothes and weapons were back at the boarding house. So he would have to make do. Hell, he was half Indian; he'd improvise.

The afternoon was almost gone, but it stayed light much longer this far north. That would give him time to make camp, maybe find some food. He looked in the trunk. The former owner had left some binder twine there from some tie-down job. Quickly he fashioned a snare and planted it along a small game trail.

By the time he had his little camp set up beside the car, he heard noises and found a fat rabbit had volunteered to be his dinner. He picked a slouch hat full of blackberries, then looked for matches. He didn't have any, so used the cigarette lighter in the Bronco to start his fire. The wood he gathered had been the dryest possible, to make the most smoke-less fire. Any wood will make smoke, but he wanted as little as possible filtering through the tall fir tree tops. He cooked half of the rabbit and ate it, but kept the rest for the following day. It would stay fresh overnight. Just before it got dark he reset his snare and made another.

Then he ate the berries. They stained his fingers, but that didn't matter. His disguise, how could he work on that? The thought came again, as a bum. So he would have a growing in beard and shorter hair. He took out his trusty Buck knife and began cutting his hair, chopping it close and uneven. No big loss, it would grow out. Next came the tougher job on his moustache.

He found water at a nearby bubbling stream, heated it in a hub cap over the fire and soaked his moustache thoroughly, then with the razor sharp Buck shaved off his lip brush. He felt odd without it, but the moustache too would grow back. He would have a full-face start of a beard that would change his appearance in two days. Mark was glad that the Welsh side of the family had provided him with strong beard-growing genes.

His eyes. They were the same. Then he checked in the car and found his sunglasses. With them and with some eye shadow ... He looked at his hands. The berry stain was still there. He picked some more berries and kept them for the next day, when he would paint deep, dark circles under his eyes. That would do it. Then he'd get his pants filthy, tear one knee, leave his flannel shirt in the car and rip his T-shirt, after getting it lived-in-dirty. The effect might work. He made a bed in the back of the Bronco, stacking up some old logs to rest his feet on out the open door, and at last got to sleep.

Three days later, Mark edged into town, paused in front of the general store and saw the owner come boiling out with a baseball bat.

"Get away from my store, you trash. Don't litter up my steps! Clear out of town. Go back where you come from." Mark ducked and limped off. He had fooled one man.

His black beard stubbled his face. His eyes looked half-dead, and he had carefully dirt-painted his face and neck, putting dirt creases on his elbow. He was dirty, ragged in the torn T-shirt, and he even smelled ripe.

Mark looked around, apparently confused, then headed for the Timber Bar two doors down. He almost knocked over somebody coming around the building. It was Al Stark.

"Why don't you watch the hell where you're going," Stark said.

"Oh, yeah?" Mark challenged, standing up, staring down at the smaller man.

Stark's angry expression faded.

Mark laughed. "Sorry, man. Lend me a buck, can you? I need me a beer."

"Get lost, I'm on the road too. But not staying around this hellhole any longer. We lost another one last night. God, I saw it this time, saw the whole goddamned thing! They got old Harry. Harry just came into town that morning. Damn shame. Harry was all alone in the world. He had nobody, and he was a crier, telling everyone about it. Harry was a convincing bastard. He even got to me. *I* loaned him a dollar. I had to after I heard his story. Last night, see, I had to get up to take a leak about one o'clock. I came out from behind this tree and I heard the chopper landing. Harry was hustled out of the Timber Bar by two big guys. One of 'em was Big Jack so help me. Man, if I had another ten I'd blow this place fast!"

"Who's this Big Jack?"

"You just get in town? Must have. Stay away from him; he's a guy who shanghais people. Never gonna talk to that son of a bitch again. Fact, I think I'll move out right now!"

Mark leaned closer to Stark. "Hey, don't I know you? How about from Williams Lake or Kamloops?"

Stark frowned and moved back. "Hell, no. I never mess around with dirty bums like you. Get lost!"

Mark walked away, limping, shambling aimlessly, but in the general direction of the

Timber Bar. He heard Stark yell something from behind him but that was all. It was about noon. He poked his head inside the bar, then went on in. The short, bald barkeep glanced at him with disgust.

"You got any money?"

"Damn ... damn right." Mark held up a torn, smudgy Canadian dollar bill. "Got me a whole dollar. How many beers that buy me, the cheapest?"

"One and change."

"Make it two and you got yourself a buck." Mark had been slurring his words, putting half a southern accent into them, hamming it up like crazy, but the barkeep obviously didn't recognize Mark.

The bartender shrugged, slid two draft beers to Mark, who guzzled one without stopping, then held the other and walked around the small place. It had six tables, two booths and a six-man stand up bar. The rotund apron tapped Mark on the shoulder.

"Listen, bum, try to mooch just one beer in here and I'll throw your ass right out in the dirt. You got that? I don't care how big you are; I can get lots of help. Remember, no goddamned mooching in here."

Mark nodded solemnly and held his beer, walking unsteadily to the table, sitting down with a smile of supreme accomplishment. A moment later he laid his head on his arms and put one hand firmly on the beer mug, pretending to sleep.

Five minutes later a bevy of loggers drifted in, laughing, swearing, still in loud flannel shirts, calk boots, jeans with ragged, cut-off cuffs that wouldn't snag in the woods and held up by suspenders. They were as dry as half of the province. The barkeep kept busy, setting up beers for them, making change and moving the dart board.

Mark saw Big Jack come in, look around, pass over him quickly, then glance back after he had inventoried the room. Mark's eyes drifted shut. Would the big man recognize him? Mark roused himself, took a short shot of his beer and stumbled clumsily to his feet. He weaved toward Big Jack.

"Hey, man, you the boss? Must be the boss, only one that's clean. I used to set chokers down in Oregon."

Big Jack looked him over, disgust obvious on his shaved, washed and aftershave-scented face. Then his expression changed.

"Hunting work, huh? How long you been looking?"

"For true, man? Going on about ... well, let's say two years."

"So you're a road rat, a knight of the highways, a bum."

"Oh, no, sir. I beg to differ with you!" He burped, ruining his composure. "I ... I just can't find a job good enough for me." Mark took a drink of his beer, which was almost gone.

Big Jack grinned. "And I bet you try damn hard."

"Yeah, like a bitch! Told this buddy of mine at Calgary once that I can do any damn job they ask me to. Can, too. So far not many have asked me to do a damn thing. Had a job in Vancouver once, for three days, loading lumber on boxcars."

"Why not just head back home?" Jack asked, his eyes sharp, watchful.

"Home? You bullshittin' me? Wherever I drop my ass is home, man. Folks both dead. No brothers. One sister in Ontario, but she don't talk to me no more." Mark almost kept the tear from slipping down his cheek.

The big man walked around him. "Hell, you look strong enough. Maybe I can get you on as a whistle punk or something in the woods. Want another beer?"

"Oh, yeah, I need one more beer, good old suds!" At the bar the apron drew two more, made a note on a tab, and shoved the beers across the bar. They both leaned back, Mark pulled on the suds and grinned.

"Shore do 'preciate your friendly gesture, friend."

"No sweat. I'm Jack; you got a name?"

"Well, of course," Mark said, pulling himself up tall, squaring his shoulders. He had stashed all of his I.D. and the money belt in a safe place in the car. "I'm Willia——Will ——call me Bill."

When the beer was gone, Jack lowered his

voice. "Look, you got a better shirt than that, or a coat? You'll freeze your balls off outside tonight. Got a hotel room?" Mark nodded.

"Like hell. I mean besides in somebody's unlocked car."

"Well . . ."

"Use my room if you want. It's paid for. I got to head into the big city, Williams Lake."

Mark finished his beer.

"Well, what you think? Like to use my digs or not? Don't mean a damn thing to me."

Mark looked at the man curiously. "Well . . . why? You don't know me, never met me before ten minutes ago."

"Son of a bitch! Can't a guy just offer somebody something free for once, without getting chewed out about it?"

Mark softened his stare. "Hell, I was just wondering . . . I mean I don't want you to think that I'm . . . I'm queer . . . gay."

Big Jack exploded in laughter. Half a dozen men in the place looked up. He quieted down and spoke softly to Mark. "Look, I don't give a shit if you're queer or not, 'cause I'm not and I'm not going to be there. If you want the place, fine, if not, butt out."

Mark downed the last of the suds and grinned. "Just checking, man. I've had to jump out of more than one window or fight, and I'd rather jump. If your place got a roof and walls, you're on."

Big Jack nodded, seeming to care little one way or the other.

"Okay, just one night though, and don't steal nothing. I know what I got. I find anything missing, I'll break your ass. I'm on my way to pack, want to come up and look at the place?"

Mark nodded, and they walked out of the tavern and across to Mrs. Loomis's boarding house.

"You live here?"

"Only place in town. Not much, but it's home. Come on up."

Things were moving faster than Mark had expected. Was this a warmup or the real game? He wasn't worried, but if this was it, he was a sheep being led to the slaughter. He just wanted to be sure he wasn't the one in the killing chute.

Big Jack opened his door and went inside. Mark followed. The room looked about the way it had before. Mark felt he should make some comment.

He looked around. "Yeah, a real bed. Wow, haven't seen one of those in a while." Mark turned away from the man. He had to play it dumb—and wait. He had started to turn back when he saw something descending toward his head. Mark tried to roll with the blow, but even as he did, he realized it wasn't going to be enough. Something slammed into his head, and he saw strange colored lights blinking on and off behind his already closed eyelids. He was falling, then it was all over, and he floated away, floated toward a long cave. As soon as he entered the cavern somebody turned out the lights.

Chapter 8

QUICK FLIGHT TO TERROR

When Mark came back to consciousness, he was helpless, tied wrist and ankle, blindfolded and gagged. It was an expert gag, one with enough bulk in his mouth so he couldn't scream, yet not enough to make him throw up and perhaps drown on his own vomit. He tried to work out of his bindings. No way. Mark had no idea how long he had been out. The Penetrator was not sure if he could sense light through the blindfold.

He took half a dozen deep breaths to help calm himself. The crack on his head hurt, but it would go away. He tried to think it through. Odds were he hadn't been unconscious long—ten, maybe fifteen minutes at the most. So it was still daylight. Probably about noon. He lay very still, but he could hear nothing. This must be part of the grabber routine, but why were they hijacking people? To work in some secret mine? Or maybe some kind of mules for narcotics? An idea crossed his mind but it evaporated before he could grasp it. Wait. All he could do now was wait.

Mark tried to sleep. He was on something

soft, the bed probably. At last he slept. He woke. He slept again.

Much later he woke and heard someone in the room, muted voices, two of them. Someone jerked his feet off the bed and strong hands lifted him upright. His ankles were untied, and he was propelled out of the room, walking in spite of himself.

Along the hall, down the stairs, almost falling, then outside. He heard the *whup-whup-whup* of the helicopter as soon as they went through the front door. He had guessed right. At least he was going to get a free chopper ride. He'd find out what happened to the "grabbed" men at least, and he hoped it was tied in with Johnny Utah. But now all he could do was hope.

They handed Mark into the chopper like a heavy bag of grain, and stretched him out on the floor. At least one more man got in the craft with him. That made three of them, including the pilot, who must have been at the controls as the bird idled.

Then they lifted off and were flying. He didn't know how long or which direction they went. North, he guessed, as Stark had told him, but would they continue north? He felt the turn, but couldn't decide what direction they were headed. He gave up trying to figure it out. Mark knew he couldn't sleep. His mind was working again. The range of most helicopters is short, two hundred miles at the average, so they wouldn't be in the air long.

The slowdown and descent came quickly. How long had it been, fifteen minutes? They landed; the engine shut off, and the rotor wound down.

As soon as he was unloaded, his gag and blindfold came off. It was dark, only a few lights showed. He could see nothing. Handling him roughly, they led him a hundred yards through a small patch of trees, then he was pushed forward and fell on his hands and knees. His hands were cut free but he lay where he had fallen. He heard a heavy door slam shut and a bar drop in place.

Mark squinted in the darkness, realizing the blur was from the tight wrap around his eyes which had distorted his eyeballs. A few moments later he could see clearly and he found himself in a cagelike wooden box, eight feet square. It looked as if it had been made of two-by-fours and four-by-fours, all rough-cut lumber set six inches apart, with many cross members. The cage looked strong enough to hold a rampaging grizzly bear.

He saw that there was more of the same on each side and guessed there were five or six such pens. Mark realized there was someone else in the next cubicle, but he couldn't see clearly. Before he could move a bright light slashed into his eyes.

"Strip!" The command came from outside.

"You can go to hell!"

Something hit him in the shoulder, an elec-

105

tric shock which jolted him backward, a tingling continuing through his body, a ringing in his ears. It had knocked him down. Mark stood, and again the command came from the darkness behind the light to take off his clothes.

Mark realized whoever held the light also had some kind of an electric prod, much stronger than the cattle prods used in the slaughterhouses or the ones cops used in street riots. The Penetrator knew whoever had the prod could touch him time and time again, no matter where he was in the pen. There might be more than one of them. He shrugged and pulled off his torn T-shirt, pants and shorts, then his shoes.

"Throw your rags over there by the gate," the voice said. The light moved to the target spot and held until the clothing hit it. Then the light returned to Mark's eyes.

"Do what you're told the first time, and you'll get along here. You don't, and you'll wish to Christ you were never born."

The light went out, the steps retreated, and Mark was alone. He looked around, knowing he could work up his *Sho-tu-ça* night sight, but refrained from it. He would save the ancient Cheyenne dog soldier's medicine-man psych-up for later. He would gain little using it now, since it would be light soon. At least he had found out what they did with the victims they grabbed: stripped them and penned them up like animals.

Although it was the first week in September, the weather was not as cold that night as Mark thought it would be. He sat at the back of his cage and listened. His sensitive hearing told him there were others on each side of him. He didn't know how many more. Mark crouched out of the wind and listened again. Someone was very near.

"Hey, where are we? What is this place?" Mark asked in a stage whisper.

"No talking!" The command came immediately, harsh, demanding.

"Fuck you!" a new voice said from Mark's right.

Two pistol shots blazed in the night, and again from the right he heard a short laugh.

"Missed me, you son of a bitch."

The shots would be high on purpose, Mark knew.

The last went unpunished, and things quieted down. Mark couldn't sleep. He was surprised how sheltered the area was. It was cool, but not painfully cold to a naked person. It seemed ten degrees warmer here than at Twist Lake. Perhaps they had flown south. How far? He tried to remember details of the map he had studied. Most of the primitive area was south of Twist Lake. If Johnny Utah was behind this and wanted privacy, surely he would have gone south, not north as Al Stark said.

Mark worried it another two hours, then dawn blushed the east. That was where east was, he noted. Soon there was enough light to see by.

There were six cages, joined with common walls on the sides. They were stronger than he had thought. No chance at all to break out, and he had none of his explosive gadgets to help him. There was another building ten yards in front, a kind of quickly built shack, probably for their keepers. Around them he saw only the virgin, British Columbia rain forest.

On one side he could see two naked men in their cells. On the other side lay the end cage of the row, and in it huddled a woman. She too was naked, but he couldn't tell her age. She sat on the dirt floor, knees drawn up, arms hugging them, head resting on her knees and her long blonde hair cascading down over her. He stepped toward the woman, but she seemed to still be sleeping.

On the other side he saw a medium-height thin man, with a growing-in beard and black hair. He stood, walked to the gate and urinated on it, then came over and lifted his brows when he saw Mark.

"So you're the new guest. A big one. Welcome to cage city."

The man was in his early twenties and walked with a decided limp. Now Mark saw he was needle thin. "Thought I heard some commotion last night. Know where you are?"

Mark shook his head. The man pointed beyond the front of the cages.

"Look through the trees, and you can see water. That's Chilko Lake, a big mother, and the very center of this wilderness. You won't find a house, a road, a logger, not even a telephone pole or hiking trail within fifty miles of here—in any direction. This is either a wilderness retreat, or the worst godforsaken hole on earth."

Mark moved to the common two-by-four barred partition and held out his hand. "My name's Bill. What the hell is this all about?"

"You don't know?" The man smiled, his green eyes snapping. "No, I guess you wouldn't. Almost none of you do when you first get here. But it becomes obvious soon enough. Like the little girl next to you there. She thought she was coming on a fishing trip. Got here a week ago. First day here she got raped by several of the men. The secret to staying alive around here is to have some infirmity, like my limp. It isn't that bad, but I make out like it's ten times worse than it really is. Then I won't eat their goddamned food, and they're afraid I'm gonna starve."

"Why? Why are we here?"

The man looked at Mark, sadness settling over his features. He sighed. "You really haven't figured it out yet? There are six cages, and all are full: a complete cast of different types and different sexes. Old and young. You really don't have a clue about this?"

"No. I just got shanghaied last night."

"Well, my friend you are in for a few surprises. All of us except the girl were kidnapped and brought here. This is, as you may know, a hunter's paradise. We have moose, deer, elk, a few antelope, black and brown bear, grizzly, wolf, fox, mountain lions, all sorts of game birds and coyotes. But we six are not here to go hunting. No, these men want a deadlier, smarter game than the natural beast. So they bring us in. Most of us are loners; no one will miss us. We are the human targets for their sport! We are the game, and they are out to bag the one 'head' most of them have never shot, a human being!"

Chapter 9

THE 100 POINT KILL

The Penetrator watched the man through the wooden bars. He was deathly serious. Suddenly many small facts that Mark had been puzzled about fell into place. The seclusion, the "grabber," the hunter element. It all made sense and sounded exactly like what the jaded Johnny Utah would do.

"The girl too? Is she a target?"

"You bet. She's special. Some big shot wants her out of the way. He brought her here."

Mark moved to the far side of the cage nearest the girl and began talking to her. His voice was soft, gentle. He told her that if he got out he would try to help her. She didn't respond. He went back to the other fence where the man sat in the dirt.

"Who in hell is behind this whole thing?"

"You don't know that, either?" The man spat at an "X" he had scratched in the dirt. He hit it in the center. "A son of a bitch by the name of Johnny Utah, a heavy mobster from Detroit. He doesn't have any Mafia connections I've heard, but the word is out that he runs everything there: dope, girls,

111

numbers, book, protection, murder for hire—
any damn thing you want. This is his hobby.
He likes to shoot people."

"Not just to shoot them, to *hunt* them,"
Mark said. "Johnny Utah is a big game
hunter, world class type. He must want a
new challenge."

"Yeah, man, that's it." He cocked his
head. "Hey, who are you? You somebody
special?" His voice lowered. "Yeah, bet
you're some kind of a cop."

Mark said he wasn't, then asked about the
limp. "You mean because of your limp you
haven't been picked as a target?"

"Right, man. I claim I can't run, can
hardly walk. I'd be no damn good as a con-
testant; I'd be a sitting duck. I don't even
eat the food they bring. Sometimes I'm so
weak I can just barely drag around. No lie. I
figure it's better to be half starved all the
time than healthy one day and shot full of
holes the next."

"I can agree with that," Mark said. "Tell
me the procedure."

"Procedure? Christ, you must be a cop.
You'll know the damn procedure soon
enough. We eat about six A.M., then they
parade out the hunter of the day, and he
takes his pick of the next caged target for
the meat grinder."

"Just like that?"

"Hell, yes. So look unhealthy. I've been

working that for almost a month now, and I'm still here, man."

A guard came out of the shack, checked the cages, then rested his M-16 on the ground and munched on a sandwich. Five minutes later a wheeled cart rolled in with breakfast. Mark was amazed at the food. It was served on army style trays, and slid under a two-inch high slot below the gate. His tray had plate sized hotcakes with butter and maple syrup, three fried eggs, a breakfast steak, hash browns, orange juice, toast, coffee and milk. Mark had seconds on the steak and hotcakes.

The thin man in the next cage shook his head. "That's no way to get sick. They keep a record of what you eat." He threw most of his food out through the door of his cell and walked over to the common bars between them. "Hey, Bill, just in case I do get out of here and you don't, or the other way around, my name is Willet, Lew Willet. I'm from Toronto."

"Bill Blank, Calgary. What happens next?"

"They give us ten minutes or so to settle our breakfast, then out comes the mighty hunter." He turned to the left and sat down quickly. "Change in schedule, somebody is coming. Go into your act, man."

Lew began shaking as if he had palsy, first his head, then one hand. He leaned back limply against the bars.

To his left Mark saw three men. Two carried rifles, the third, dressed in slacks and a wild sport shirt, looked familiar. Mark scanned his memory of the pictures he had seen in the professor's file of Johnny Utah and made the connection. There he was, the Detroit kingpin and target of this whole caper—only right then Mark knew *he* was still the target.

Utah toured the cages from the far end. He made short remarks to one of the guards, who carried a clipboard and pen. At Lew's cage he shook his head. "Not him," Johnny said and moved on to stare at Mark.

"Well, this one is healthy. You're new. Big enough, but have you got any guts?"

"Enough to take you any day, Utah."

The man didn't seem to notice the jibe. "Put a favorable mark behind this one, but save him. He sounds interesting."

Johnny walked on to the girl's cage. She had moved very little, still covered herself with her arms and hair. Utah laughed.

"Honey, I like you better flat on your back. You're a hell of a lot more fun that way. Don't worry, this ain't your day." He laughed and walked back down the line of cages, then disappeared into the woods to the left.

Slowly Lew stopped his shaking. When he was sure the mobster wasn't coming back, he looked over at Mark and grinned. "Damn I should at least get a nomination for an academy award for that acting job. Wasn't I great! I got a reprieve for another day. But what the hell were you doing standing up there baiting him? That just makes him mad and you'll go high on the list. He suggests each day who the hunter should pick. The hunter still has a choice, but old Johnny suggests."

"How does this little game work? Any rules?"

"Their rules. The hunter is armed, the victim is not. The target has an hour head start. The hunter has binoculars. All you have to do is stay alive for forty-eight hours, and you win your freedom. That's what Utah says, but he can't afford to let any of us leave here alive. We know it, and he sure does. That $25,000 and an airline ticket to South America is just a come on, a con game to make the *animals* fight harder for their lives."

"What weapons do they use?"

Lew snorted. "Anything they want to. But they have to take along a knife, a pistol, a fully automatic M-16 or other rifle, and a bow and arrow with broad hunting tips."

Before he could say anything else the man in the far cage coughed. It was the signal and Lew slumped again and went into his shaking act. Mark stood at the front of his cell and watched the procession. In front came one of the short stout men who had been with Johnny. He carried weapons.

Striding along behind him was a man Mark guessed was six-foot-six. He had a full head of blond hair and a blond moustache. The man weighed at least two hundred fifty pounds, Mark guessed, and none of it was fat. He looked to be about thirty.

Behind him came another man loaded with binoculars, canteen, the bow and arrows and small back pack evidently filled with food and equipment. Trailing him, was Johnny Utah, smiling broadly. The hunter looked in each cage. He paused at Mark's cell, then went back to another.

"Welcher Mann?" he asked Johnny.

Johnny turned to the man with the bow.

"He wants to know which one you would suggest?"

Johnny looked at the pens and pointed to the second one from the far end.

The big German's head bobbed. *"Ja,* me too."

Mark watched in a strange kind of suppressed horror as the man was led from the cage. The man would soon be dead. Executed for sport! He was naked, without weapons, bearded, and for just a moment the German stared into the man's eyes.

"Ich machte dir denn Garaus!" (I'm going to kill you!) he said.

Johnny Utah pushed the target on the shoulder. "Get your ass out of here," he snapped. "You've only got fifty-nine minutes

116

left before this expert killer comes after your stinking hide."

The man ran.

He raced behind the cages and into the thick brush and timber. The German watched him with a sneer.

Later, after a conversation with Johnny Utah, he slid his heavy arms into the pack straps and adjusted the web belt around his waist. This now held the army style canteen and a U.S. rifle bayonet in a scabbard. The German checked the M-16, shook his head and reached instead for a hunting rifle with scope. Mark saw now that the web belt also had a holster, something small, probably for a .32 pistol. The German slung the bow over his back, tied the arrows together and had his helper push them carefully into the pack. Then he sat down and closed his eyes. Thirty minutes later Johnny came back to the cages and fired a pistol. The German took three long pulls from a pint of whiskey, had it refilled and added that to his pack as well.

That was when Mark noted that the hunter's clothing was all green camouflaged. The rifle barrel had been dulled,—nothing shone or sparkled on the man or equipment. He looked like a commando going on a mission.

Johnny looked at his watch. "Five minutes early, but what the hell?" He motioned with his hand, and the interpreter beside him said something. The German saluted Johnny as if he were a general and walked with long strides into the woods where the human prey had vanished.

Those outside the cages began making bets on how long it would take him to kill the victim. Most of the betting centered around twenty to twenty-two hours. They walked away to the left, where Mark guessed there must be a camp.

"Camp?" Willet asked in surprise. "No it's more like a luxurious hunting lodge. Huge palace with ten bedrooms, big kitchen, fireplace, dining room, the works. Got his own generator for electricity. Flies in the diesel to keep the generator motor going, and that's it."

"He planned ahead."

Willet shook his head. "Naw, place has been here for years. Some rich society dame used to own it. This guy bought it from her."

"The man who went ... the human target. How long was he here?"

Lew thought a moment. "Oh, yeah, that was old Harry. He came in one, maybe two days ago. He's cashing in his chips damn quick."

Mark felt the edge of frustration threatening him.

"Are you positive there's no way out of here? A weak spot? How about a tunnel?"

"Forget it. Every man here has tried. The two-by-fours go down two feet in the dirt.

And there's no way to cover up a tunnel if you start one."

Mark slumped back, sitting on the bare ground, staring straight ahead. There was nothing he could do for Harry. He must be the same man Stark saw loaded on the chopper at Twist Lake two nights ago. Now what came next? Who next?

"Lew, why all the weapons? One M-16 is better than all the rest of that arsenal."

"Rules. Hey, that's right. You don't know the rest of the regulations. This is a game, right? If the killer makes an unarmed score on the target, he gets a hundred points and another go-round. If it's a knife kill, he gets seventy-five points, and then fifty points for a bow and arrow kill and twenty-five counters for a pistol wipe-out. If he uses a rifle, he gets only five points.

"A deadly game," Mark said, angry that one human being could do this to another, but recognizing the underworld butcher type. "Who are the hunters?"

"Only seen a few. I'd guess some buddies of Johnny Utah from the rackets. One or two international types, who must be from European crime factories. I hear some pay $50,-000 to play."

"What about the girl? Why is she a target?"

"Don't know much. One of the guards said she was a former girlfriend of some big shot in New York. She heard or saw something she shouldn't and threatened to yell cop. So now she's here as a target, just like the rest of us. Only she's reserved. Don't ask me why."

Mark sat there, a frown building on his craggy face. He couldn't do anything while he was in this cage. He had to get out. The quickest way was to make sure he was the next human target. That was it!

Once he was set free he would have a chance to outwit the hunter who came after him, and get the man's weapons. Then Mark knew he could attack the lodge, storm it, burn it down, do something.

Mark stood up and went to the front of the cage. He began screaming and shouting. A moment later a guard appeared with a long wooden-handled metal pole connected to a suitcase gadget with wires on it. Mark guessed it was the electric prod he had felt last night.

"Shut up!" the guard screamed. "Quiet, or I'll fry you, asshole!"

"Shut up yourself," Mark growled back. "Go get Johnny Utah down here. I can tell him a hell of a lot about a guy who is starting to move in on his heroin operation in Detroit. And tell him I know all about that twin cop-kill in that Detroit alley."

The guard stopped, debated with himself, then put the equipment away and hurried off.

"Man, you crazy?" Lew asked from the

other cage. "Don't draw attention to yourself. Don't make waves."

"Sure, and get wiped out," he said to Lew, then went on screaming that he wanted to talk to Utah. Mark stopped and went to the far corner of his cage, squatted down for a moment, then came back to the front of the cell and screamed some more. Two minutes later Johnny Utah boiled onto the scene. He had a pistol with him, and when he saw it was Mark who was screeching, he walked forward more slowly, stopping eight feet from the wooden bars.

Mark's right hand was behind him, where it had been since he moved to the bars from the cage corner.

Utah glared at the Penetrator. "What's this shit about some cops getting killed in Detroit?"

"You know all about it, Utah; you did it. Probably a payoff for two more boys on the pad. You probably used a hot loaded .45 or maybe a magnum .44. But you pulled the trigger."

Utah lowered his pistol and laughed. His head went back, and his eyes closed. Mark pushed his hands through the bars and threw what he had been holding. Mark's bowel movement that morning had been soft and his hand had warmed it more. The handful of excrement hit Johnny Utah in the chest, splattered over his face, staggering him backward. The pistol went off six times in random directions, triggered by blind fury. Johnny Utah gagged, screamed, then fell to his knees and threw up.

Mark saw the guards coming. Three buckets of water splashed on him and he saw two of the long aluminum cattle prods jabbing into his cell, one from each side. The water soaked him and the dirt floor and made a perfect electrical ground for the prods. It intensified the power, and the first touch on his bare shoulder knocked him down. The second touch rolled him one way on the muddy cell floor. The next convulsed him in the opposite direction, then both touched him at once and he couldn't keep the scream tearing from his throat. Mark's eyes snapped open then, and he tried to utilize his *Sho-tu-ça*. But it was too late; he didn't have time. He saw Johnny Utah still retching, trying to throw up his guts.

The prods hit him again and again, and he wondered how high the charges were, how many volts he was taking. He knew no matter how furious Utah was, he wouldn't let them kill him. He was sure he would live long enough to be the next target. Tomorrow.

It had been a risk, a carefully calculated one that the Penetrator had taken. Johnny might have killed him on the spot, but he hadn't. The idea was to infuriate the hoodlum to such a point that he would be the next target. Mark could do nothing as long as he was weaponless and trapped inside the cage.

He had to take any drastic measures to get out. The sooner he got out, the quicker innocent people in the other cages would stop dying. He firmed his resolve and held in the scream the next time the prods touched him with liquid fire.

Chapter 10

SPEAR THE MAN DOWN

Mark Hardin lost all track of time. The prods kept touching him, jolting him, making him coil up and writhe from numbing, slashing pain. Toward the last, Utah had recovered and was using a prod, cursing at him, screaming, and now and then shooting his pistol, the bullets splattering so near Mark that mud and dirt sprayed into his face, though no lead touched him.

At last even the Penetrator's strong constitution could take no more, and he passed out. Buckets of water roused him for more torture, then suddenly it was over. Through heavy fog he heard Utah speaking.

"Whoever the hell you are," Utah said, "it don't matter. By this time tomorrow you'll be buzzard meat."

He pushed the stunning prod into Mark's crotch and laughed wildly as the Penetrator screamed and rolled away from the bars, unconscious once more.

Much later Mark came awake. It was dark. He felt the dozens of tortures on his naked body, where the electric prods had burned him. All he wanted now was sleep,

sleep and more sleep. Mark rolled over on his back not caring about the mud of the pen's dirt floor and mercifully went to sleep again.

At six o'clock the next morning three shots woke him. The blasts came from nearby in the brush and seconds later the tall German came into camp. Mark sat up painfully and tried to watch. The guards crowded around the man until he pushed them aside. Then he marched slowly, directly in front of the cages. He was so close to the bars on the far end that Mark couldn't see him. Mark heard shouts and moans down the line, then the German was in front of Willet's cage, and Mark could see.

The big blond man held his bayonet upright in his massive right hand, and stabbed on the end of the knife was a human head—old Harry's. Mark stared into the German's eyes and saw only blood lust. The Penetrator scowled, staring down the German, making him look away, and Mark saw the treacherous smirk fade a little, then evaporate, and the bayonet start to lower.

Mark pulled his thoughts back to his mission: first to get out of this damn cage and survive, then to waste Johnny Utah.

This was his day! He was getting out today, and he would begin to settle accounts with this butcher, this Johnny Utah. But first he had to get ready. He began with eyes closed, saying the ancient soft Cheyenne words, thought the hard thoughts and put his body into the *Sho-tu-ça* ceremonial trance. He worked hard with his mind for several minutes, cleansing, purifying it, and soon he felt the beginnings of the new energy, the rejuvenation of his body, and a surge of psychological power. It flashed through his veins like adrenaline. That could be what it was, Mark did not know, nor did he question the old rite his fellow tribesman David Red Eagle had taught him. He knew his body must pay for this surge of power later. But then he could afford to recoup and rest.

Mark jumped to his feet and yelled insults at the German, then screamed for Johnny Utah to come out. One of the guards ran toward Mark with his electric prod and jabbed it through the bars toward Mark. The Penetrator feinted one way, then slashed at the clumsy prod with the side of his hand. The thundering karate blow bent the three-quarter-inch diameter aluminum tube in half and tore it from the guard's hands, ripping the wires on it from the charging unit. The guard yelped and jumped backward.

Mark picked up the dead prod and bent and smashed it into a jumbled mass, then threw it, hitting the guard in the chest.

Johnny Utah came charging onto the scene and stared at the ruined prod.

"That guy should be half dead by now," Johnny yelled at the guard. He turned toward Mark.

The Penetrator kicked his breakfast tray of food back through the slot under the door. Johnny walked down, hands on his hips, and stared at Mark.

"Should I know you? Are you from Detroit?" Johnny asked.

"Not from Bloomfield Hills, that's for damn sure. You've never even stopped in Hazel Park or Ferndale. You're too busy chasing those other queers out in Cranbrook and Birmingham. I understand you're a goddamned gay son-of-a-bitch. You probably enjoyed that present I gave you last night, you shithead."

Utah bristled, looked for the other electric prod, but abandoned the idea. He pulled his .45 pistol from his hip holster. "You won't run so fast today, with a bullet in your leg, dumb ass!" Johnny lifted the gun. Mark did not flinch, didn't move or cower back. Johnny put the .45 away.

"Hell, no. I'll wait on that. You're the target today, big mouth. I'll send my best man after you, and tonight we'll have a banquet and your head will be right in the middle of the fucking table on a silver platter. We'll see what you have to say then!"

He turned abruptly and marched back toward the lodge.

Mark smiled. Now he knew for sure he would be out today, and with or without a bullet in him, he would defeat anyone they sent against him. A one-on-one game would be a snap.

Lew Willet in the cage beside Mark tapered off his palsy shaking and whistled softly. "Damn, I knew you were somebody special, but I didn't think Superman. How did you take all those shocks and come back this way? Last guy they jolted that much died right in his cage. Utah was really pissed about that. Who the hell are you, anyway?"

"Right now I'm a man trying to stay alive," Mark said.

"And you're going to do it by going up against a rifle, a pistol, a bow and arrow and a knife?"

Mark didn't answer. He sat down at the back of the cage in the one dry spot and continued his *Sho-tu-ça* ritual, trying to intensify his senses, especially his sight and hearing.

Lew shook his head, amazed. "I just don't know, maybe you can do it. Never saw anybody knock down a prod the way you did. Was that karate? Man but you are cool. Coolest guy I ever saw."

Five minutes later Mark's cage door was unlocked and he stepped through it to freedom. He would not get an hour's start. A hunter stood five feet from him, outfitted with his weapons and pack. That would slow the man's reactions. Two guards stood by with rifles, but not pointed at Mark.

"You get five minutes head start," Utah

said. "Then Jones is coming after you. He never misses."

"Utah, you come after me," Mark said. "Afraid?"

"Hell no. I promised Jones the next hunt. I never go back on a promise. You're nothing special. I'm waiting for an Eskimo, now that would be sport. You're too easy."

Mark tensed himself, seeing his chance. The hunter had taken his eyes off Mark for a split second, and that's when Mark leaped forward, his right hand slashing out with all of his strength, smashing against Jones's throat. The side handed blow crushed the trachea, ruptured the right carotid artery and thundered forward, snapping the man's long thin neck, killing him instantly.

Before Johnny Utah could draw his pistol Mark had charged directly over him, knocking him down, spilling the revolver into the dirt and scattering the two guards on either side, who were trying to bring up their long guns for a close-in shot. The Penetrator sprinted ten yards for the rear of the cages, hearing one shot go off, then surged around the cage, putting the wide two-by-fours and four-by-fours between him and the rifles.

Ten yards and two futile shots later, Mark plunged into the protective cover of the brushy woods. He ran full speed at his ten-second-flat hundred-yard pace until he had covered the three hundred feet, then slowed to a six-minute mile speed, crashing through brush and past trees, crossing a small creek and then veering to his left. He followed the terrain, not climbing the hill directly behind the camp, but quartering the slope, neither going up or down it and making good time. He splashed through another stream, stopped and scooped up a hand-sized piece of jagged blue flint. He dropped it. If he had time he could make a spear point or a crude knife, but time he didn't have.

His sudden attack had thrown the cage guards into a panic, as he hoped it would. He knew the hunter was dead. Now it would take them a half hour to outfit another hunter to come after him. Maybe Johnny himself would come, but Mark doubted it. Mark heard the helicopter after ten minutes, but he kept to well forested areas so he could not be spotted from the bird.

He ran for an estimated thirty minutes, which meant he should be five miles from the lodge. Then he drank from a clear stream; he wished he could make a spear point. He looked at the trees and brush. He needed a club or a spear. It was virgin forest. A few older trees had ripened, died and fallen. In some areas he found splintered remains. Now he knew what he needed. He watched for another splintered tree, an old one. Five minutes later he found one, a cedar of some kind. Six-foot-long shafts of the splintered trunk lay in front of him. He pried one off, and tested it. Fine, but blunt on the end. He found one that was just right a few minutes later. It was four feet long, two inches thick and almost that wide. The end had splintered into a jagged point six inches long. It would work fine.

Mark discarded the idea of trying to outrun his captors. He could not outdistance the helicopter. There would be open stretches he would have to cross, and they could patrol those, or drop in permanent guards by the chopper to watch for him.

Mark sighed. It might be possible to escape to civilization if that were his purpose, but that wasn't why he had come here. He had to eliminate Johnny Utah, put an end to his sadistic mankilling game and destroy his hoodlum and heroin activity in Detroit.

If only Utah had stood a few feet closer that morning, Mark could have attacked him instead of the hunter and the work would be done. But the crafty Utah had stayed back, just far enough to be out of reach, and it had saved his life. Now, Mark would do it by the numbers. Wear down the opposition until he could move in on the top man.

Mark watched his back trail. They would try to spot him and fly in the hunter close by chopper. So he would help them. He moved into the open on a dusty hillside that had been scarred by numerous landslides. He found a spot where he could easily start a rock slide and then run into the cover of the trees before they could gun him from the chopper. Then he waited.

It was a half hour before the helicopter appeared. When it was about a half mile away, Mark started the slide, then ran across the rest of the open ground, sure they would spot him. A great cloud of dust rose from the slide, serving as a beacon for the chopper pilot and hunter. Moments later he dashed into the protection of the fir-covered mountain and waited.

The chopper zeroed in on the slide area, hovered for a moment, then moved directly to where Mark hid behind a big fir tree. The chopper backed off and settled to the ground on a flat area a quarter of a mile away. One hunter got out, and Mark saw what he thought was a hand radio set on one arm. The chopper lifted off and flew out of sight. So this was to be a modern manhunt complete with two-way radio? Mark laughed at their careful preparation. They still had to see a man before they could shoot at him.

When Mark was sure the lone hunter who came after him had found his trail, he made a blundering easy-to-follow path, breaking branches, stomping down plants. Quickly he fashioned a loop in his trail, crossing over the original track. He was far enough ahead so he waited as the hunter passed not fifty yards away. The man was not Johnny Utah nor the big German. Mark had never seen this man before, but he had the look of a big city type.

Mark went back to work, laying a new trail, again making a loop, smaller this time, only where the routes crossed he made it obvious they were crossing. Mark made a down-trail then came back carefully and spotted a half-grown fir four feet from where the paths crossed. It had thick heavy branches eight feet off the ground. Mark made sure the hunter was still on the way, then climbed the fir and positioned himself so the hunter could not see him as he approached.

Mark waited. He knew a lot about waiting. One time he had lain in a hole under a thin gauze covering in the desert's hot sun. The covering had been sprinkled with sand to make it blend with the rest of the desert. He hadn't moved for two hours, then he'd silently risen and killed two murderers who thought they were home free.

Again he waited. Soon his sensitive hearing picked up the sounds of the man working up the trail. A grin spread across the hunter's face when he spotted the cross over. This time he did not continue up and around the loop, but did what Mark knew a good hunter would, skipped the loop and began checking out the new crossing track. The hunter was directly below Mark, down on his haunches inspecting the ground.

Mark moved slightly on the branch where

he sat, then holding the spear, aimed it at the hunter and jumped. The spear point stabbed into the man's back, and with Mark's two hundred pounds of weight behind it, drove straight through lungs and heart, emerging out his chest. The man had no time to make a sound. He died instantly, crumpling to the ground, rolling over until the shaft of the spear stopped him.

Mark looked at the face, the staring death eyes. He did not know the man. He was about six feet tall, around fifty years old and had a full head of black hair. Mark pulled the light jacket off the man and put it on, then he took off the hunter's pants and got into them, tightening the belt to take up the slack around his waist. The boots didn't fit.

Mark removed a billfold from the pants pocket and checked for identification. The man was from New York, Roscoe E. Antonucci.

Mark rolled the name over in his mind, then snapped his fingers. *Toombs Antonucci*, one of the minor hoods of New York from Queens or out on the Island. A waster, Mark had heard much about Toombs. Now he would waste no one else.

Mark gathered up the weapons, all of them, and the web belt. He checked the bore of the M-16 and swore. When Antonucci had fallen, he had jammed the rifle muzzle deep into the soft earth, plugging the bore. It was worthless without a cleaning rod. Mark threw it deep into the brush, then checked the pistol, a .38 with six rounds in it. There was no radio. Either Antonucci had lost it or Mark had been mistaken. The binoculars would help, though, and the pack, which he hoped had lightweight food.

Mark loaded up and moved out, taking pains to leave absolutely no trail, no sign whatsoever. Mark wondered what the next hunter who found Toombs would think. It might put a little fear into him. Mark didn't let himself become over confident. With the chopper they wouldn't only be trail tracking. And he remembered how David Red Eagle had surprised Mark more than once when the Penetrator thought he had left a no-sign trail.

Mark tested the bow, shooting one of the hunting tipped arrows lightly into a patch of soft earth. He retrieved the arrow. Yes, it was a good bow, and would be his weapon for long range, twenty to a hundred yards, and it was silent. Anything closer he would use the .38. Mark rested under a large fir tree and listened for the chopper. He heard it faintly, then sensed it coming toward him.

He was on the edge of a shelf now, where the land dropped off abruptly on one side and rose in a cliff on the other. It was a channel. He had two choices, to go directly down the slope, or up into the higher reaches of the foothills. As he debated the chopper came closer, then seemed to wheel and move directly toward him. The helicopter was stymied here, no clear spot to land new troops.

But to Mark's surprise, a rope ladder fell from the chopper door as it hovered thirty feet off the ground. Two green-clad men with M-16 rifles over their backs swung expertly down the rope. Mark checked them with his binoculars. It's damn hard to climb down a rope ladder when that downdraft is slamming into you, he knew from experience in combat. Through the glasses Mark saw that each man had a back pack and on the front shoulder straps were fitted four hand grenades, in exactly the position Mark had used many times. Mark frowned. He was sure these two hunters were seasoned combat veterans with 'Nam experience.

Mark put down the glasses and worked his way up the shelf away from the two men below. As he did the men hit the ground and the chopper swung away, directly over his concealed hiding spot, then clattered a hundred yards north.

A moment later, below the chopper, Mark heard the familiar crunching explosion of two fragmentation grenades. Mark stopped.

They had him boxed in. He ripped off the jacket and felt along the seams. He found it in the bulky collar, a small transmitter, a sending device. Had Johnny Utah planned to sacrifice the first man so Mark would pick up and wear his field jacket with the tracking bug? Or had it been just another hedge on his bet? Mark started to smash the sender, then changed his mind. If he could leave it somewhere ... He put it on a branch of a fir tree, and taking his strung bow and adjusting the arrows so they were easy to reach in the pack, Mark moved south to meet the two experienced jungle fighters advancing on him, each with an M-16 automatic.

Chapter 11

SILENT, FLYING DEATH

Mark wished he had time to utilize the Cheyenne skills of the Wind Walker, so he could pass unnoticed past the two men, but already he heard the two jungle fighters moving in on him. He heightened his hearing again and found their positions, but both were screened from him by bushes and trees. He moved to the very edge of the dropoff and crouched near a bushy fir that was six feet tall. He nocked an arrow, knowing the near man would be the next to dash from his current cover and concealment to the next one, a clump of rocks fifteen yards ahead. One man must be covering for the other, leapfrogging ahead for protection, and hoping for surprise.

Mark saw a cautious eye peering from behind a tree at ground level where the Penetrator had guessed the closest man was. These men had good training, but not complete. In the next instant the hunter was up and running, bent over, to present a small target. Mark had drawn his arrow back when he first saw the eye. Now he followed the runner, led him with a three foot sight and released the arrow. He had guessed the bow's pull at seventy pounds. Now it drilled the arrow straight and true, catching the man just below the left shoulder in his side when his arm pumped forward as he ran. The arrow, with its wide steel dagger point sliced between ribs, slanted upward through the lung and almost cut his heart in half as it continued on into the other lung.

The mercenary stumbled, his head dropping, slamming him forward in a roll that snapped off the shaft of the arrow. He made only one small cry as he died, his M-16 flung to one side.

Mark guessed he had been the lead man. No other movement was obvious. Mark's hearing had placed the second gunman ten yards to the man's right and slightly behind. There was no chance the gunman had seen Mark, but he might have seen his partner go down.

Mark crouched behind the small fir, waiting. He had no cover if the armed man came at him on assault fire, burning the tree with deathly .223 caliber lead. But he was sure the other rifleman did not have an exact position on him. He would know the death missile came from somewhere in front, but he couldn't tell if it came from the right or the left. Mark guessed the speed of the arrow had probably kept the cover man from seeing it, so he might not even know what kind of a weapon he was up against. That would make the hunter doubly careful about making an attack on an unknown enemy with an unknown weapon that killed silently.

The Penetrator continued to wait as the stillness stretched into five minutes. The chopper seemed to be hovering to the north, and Mark heard two more *karumphing* explosions of hand grenades. There was a chance the unmoving electronic bug on the jacket would hold the chopper detector over that spot for a while, but not indefinitely.

After another five minutes, Mark heard movement; the hunter was retreating. Mark began to move cautiously with him. He looked backward at the weapons the dead man had, especially the M-16, but there was no way he could claim it. Until Mark could work an escape from this box, he had to trace the hunter to be sure he knew where he was. Mark kept far enough back to be out of sight, moved only when the man ahead did. Once he had to drop suddenly behind a log when the hunter paused longer than usual. Mark did not get a chance to shoot at him with the bow.

The retreat continued. Half a mile below, Mark found an escape route down the drop off to his left which had faded into a small gully. He scrambled down it and up the other side vanishing quickly back into the timber. As he did the helicopter swung around. An observer could have seen him, but the bird was more than half a mile away.

Mark had decided early not to stalk the rifleman with only his bow. It was not a good percentage play, he might win once out of three times, but those were not good enough odds ... He had to make the rifleman and the hunters come to him. The Penetrator left a trail again, breaking brush, making marks on the rocks in grass as if he were rushing, in a panic. The timber grew denser, until he could see only a dozen feet through the brush and thick stand of firs. The forest had been burned off in spots years ago, but here it seemed to be virgin timber, with tremendously tall first-growth fir, towering into the blue sky. Some of the trees had matured, died and been blown over and lay rotting back into the forest soil floor.

Another quarter mile ahead Mark came to what he thought was a newly fallen tree. But it hadn't crashed all the way down. Two smaller trees seemed to be holding it up. The trunk was forty feet long, over two feet thick and had broken off at the ground; now it leaned precariously on the younger trees. Neither of the younger ones could hold it up alone, but together they did the job.

Mark evaluated the shaky situation, then began working. First he found a pair of small firs about three inches in diameter and chopped them down and trimmed them with the long bayonet the first hunter had provided on his web belt. These he positioned as braces directly under the big tree, estimat-

ing their ninety degree crushability factor
and deciding they would prevent the tree
from falling. His next move was the hard
slow work of cutting one of the six-inch trees
nearly in half, but so no chips would show
and nothing would seem out of the ordinary.
He worked on the side away from the new
trail.

It took more than an hour to cut that
much, since he couldn't swing hard with the
big knife and make a loud chopping sound.
Twice he heard the chopper criss-crossing
the area. They had lost him. He would help
them find his trail again when he was ready.

Mark made one more cut on the tree and
heard a faint crack. The tree swayed back a
foot as a ton of solid fir pressed down on it.
He watched his three-inch thick braces sink
a foot deep into the ground, then the movements stopped and the tree held.

Mark planned the trigger. It couldn't be a
trip wire or key block to be kicked. This one
had to be sure. In the hunter's pack he found
a coil of one-eighth inch brown nylon line. It
was the kind often used on boats and Mark
knew it had a breaking strength of over two
thousand pounds. He remembered some of
David Red Eagle's instructions now and
painstakingly scored one of the braces.

Mark cut, then listened to the wood. He
was waiting for the slightest crack, like the
tentative breaking of the grain when a
wedge begins to split a chunk of wood, or the

142

crack of the core of a tree as the saw bites through just before it is sawed all the way in half. One more chip and Mark heard the soft breaking of a single fiber in the smaller of the braces. He had tied the nylon line carefully around the brace just over the cut. Now he finished stringing the line through the brush and trees for twenty yards, making sure he had a direct pull.

The Penetrator sat down, ate some of the dried meat from the pack and drank some canned juice. Then he camouflaged his presence, picking up every chip, lifting crushed plants and ferns, smoothing the forest mulch of hundreds of years. When that was done, he went to the clear side of the trap and designed a trail that would lead his victims directly to the deadfall.

It took Mark another hour, then he sat down and tried to pick out the best way to attract his man. There was no handy slide-prone mountain. No tracking bug. At last he laid the trail away from the deadfall, cleared a spot and built a small fire. It was big enough so the chopper would spot the smoke. He left some of the food wrappers, and one of the gloves that had been in the pack and moved back up the trail to the deadfall, checking it one last time. Yes, it would work. Mark left the pack itself under the heavy balanced tree as the perfect bait. The Penetrator went back and took out half the food from the pack, carried it with him to the end of the nylon cord trigger and waited. It took over half an hour for the chopper to spot the smoke and fly to it. Mark hoped the new man had radio communications. It was probable.

High overhead the chopper spotter had seen the smoke and advised his man on the ground to approach with caution. The radio had crackled with a 10-4 police type acknowledgement.

When he reached the campfire, the hunter never did move into the clearing. He suspected it was a trap to get him in the open for a fatal ambush. He wasn't that dumb now, any more than he had been in 'Nam for two years. Instead he circled the clearing, his eyes searching the ground.

Frank grinned as he found the trail leading away from the fire. He hoped he could move along this new track silently and come up in back of the son of a bitch watching the clearing! That way he'd take him out with a clean head shot and be back to the lodge in time for chow.

Frank Disco was a wiry man, under six feet, twenty-three, and had used two of those years learning how to kill the damned Gooks in 'Nam. One more kill wouldn't bother him a bit. He'd been working for Johnny Utah in Detroit for a year now, and when this special assignment came up, he'd grabbed it. So far it had been wild, just wild.

He frowned as he checked ahead. The trail seemed to enter a heavier wooded area. No

144

good. That damn bow and arrow man could shoot. It would give him more cover.

Frank knew he would have to check every possible ambush spot, move ahead carefully. He did. Then he spotted another broken branch ahead and shook his head. This guy had to be a city goon to leave this many signs when he walked through the woods.

Frank moved in a short dash to the next cover, a big tree near the trail, and checked again.

Ahead he saw part of a broken tree and smiled. Maybe the son of a bitch had made a camp! Wouldn't that be the shits if he could nail this guy in his sleep? Christ, he'd never snuffed anybody in his sleep, not even a Gook.

Frank looked into the brush again. There was a chance that the bastard who had killed Joe could be out there waiting for him. But, hell, nobody lived forever. He spurted ahead another fifteen feet and went flat on the ground behind a tree. Nothing. No fire, no sound, nothing. Frank got on his knees and was about to move to the next tree when he saw something ahead. Up there ten yards was a goddammed pack! That was just like the hunters used, so it must be Antonucci's. Which meant this crumb had captured the M-16 and the bow. Johnny had really been pissed when Antonucci got wasted. That's when he called out his expert executioner squad.

The pack. Damn, did this joker drop it, or leave it there because he was coming back? Maybe if he just watched it a while? The brush was too thick for a rifle shot to get through very far, even if this joker did grab that Sixteen. That meant it wasn't an ambush. Hell, he'd just move in on it, with total security, look over the damn thing. It couldn't be booby trapped, because this guy didn't have any explosives—Antonucci didn't have any with him. So what the hell, this bastard probably heard the chopper coming, pissed his pants as he ran away and forgot the damn pack. Nothing to sweat about.

Frank began crawling on alternate arms and knees, moving up from one bit of cover or concealment to the next, working slowly. He paused once, and forced himself to wait until he counted to a hundred and twenty by one-thousands—that should be two minutes. Nothing moved ahead. He began to work forward again, the M-16 cradled over his arms. His knees began to hurt. He hadn't done much of this since basic training.

He was closer now, fifteen feet ahead. He crawled toward a small tree, dodged around it and pushed over some brush. They sure didn't grow stuff very well around here.

The last ten feet he raised up, and with the M-16 at port arms in front and ready to fire, he charged up to the pack. Nothing moved. He slid to a stop on his knees beside the pack, lay his rifle in back of him and stared, close up, at the pack. But he did not touch it. Look but don't touch is a fine habit and a good way to stay alive in any combat zone.

Mark Hardin had heard rather than seen the hunter coming. The man was good. Moving, waiting, picking his cover carefully. Mark now lay flat on the ground, the nylon loop firm in his hand. He realized he would have to lunge backward with all of his strength and his two hundred pounds of weight to break off the pin of the trigger.

Mark saw his prey when the man stopped at the last tree in front of the deadfall. He was young, but alert, wary.

The Penetrator saw the man run for the pack. Mark squatted, both hands in the loop, waiting. When he saw the hunter kneel down at the pack, Mark tightened the line, then lunged backward with all of his strength and weight to pull the half-cut support pole out from under the deadfall.

Chapter 12

DEADFALL TWICE, FOR SURE

Mark felt the strain on the nylon line, sensed as it stretched to its limit, then the weakened pole cracked, pulled forward and Mark tumbled backward into the brush. The Penetrator heard the other three-inch supporting pole snap, then a *whooshing* as limbs of the big fir crashed downward before the trunk slammed into the forest floor with a jolt he could feel twenty yards away.

Through the sounds of the falling tree a long, high-pitched scream shattered the forest's natural sounds, then the voice ended abruptly. Mark scrambled to his feet. He had put the bow nearby, strung with an arrow nocked, ready to pull. Now he grabbed the weapon and moved stealthily up to the fallen fir. He could see dozens of three- and four-inch thick limbs angled toward him from the big tree. Where the back pack had been he saw only a forest of limbs and the two-foot thick tree trunk flat on the ground.

Mark worked carefully around the butt end of the tree to the other side. Fewer limbs had grown here, and Mark saw a silent form, the hunter's head and one arm showing from under the fir. —

The Penetrator moved closer. The man's eyes were glazed, open; he was not breathing. Then Mark saw the jagged four-inch stub limb that had broken off as the tree fell and the end of it had driven straight down through the hunter's chest and on into the ground below.

Then as if to make doubly sure the victim was dead, the ton of green fir log rammed down on top of the body, splattering the torso, almost smashing the body in half.

When Mark was sure the hunter was dead, he looked for the M-16. It was at one side, as if the victim had put it down before he knelt to examine the remains of the pack. Mark checked and found the weapon in perfect condition and with a full magazine. There must have been more rounds in the hunter's pockets, but they were taken out of the play by the tree. Mark hefted the familiar .223 caliber rifle with the carrying handle on top and smiled. It felt like old times—only now he was in another forest, another land and with another enemy.

The Penetrator had tremendous respect for the M-16 rifle. Although it fired a bullet only slightly larger around than the .22 rifle, its striking power was much greater because it was 37 percent heavier, 40 grains vs. 55 grains of lead, and at 3,250 feet per second it had a muzzle velocity 2.8 times as great as a .22. A magazine of the bullets could quickly chew up a cement building block.

He had been thinking about the M-16 in his hand, now he considered his situation. He saw no radio on the man, but he was sure to have a tracer bug on him. Mark took the man's boots, a little big but better than trying to hike barefoot. He grabbed the M-16, too, and making as little trail as possible, moved out, striking back toward the lake and the lodge. His real work was back there.

Mark found thickets of blackberry vines many places in the woods. He stopped and ate some of the berries, then rounded a huge growth of the tangled vines and their sprawling, tentaclelike runners when he heard a strange sound, a kind of mewing, almost a moan. Mark circled the rest of the bush with the M-16 up.

It was a small bear cub. The little animal had rolled and tangled itself in the prickly, thorn-laden vines and couldn't move. Mark had no idea what kind of a bear it was, but this one was harmless. The little bear couldn't have weighed twenty pounds and was about the size of a cocker spaniel. It was not nearly big enough yet to be outside of the den.

Mark pulled his bayonet and began cutting away the spiked blackberry vines, unwinding them from the small bear that had no fear at all of this strange, new animal helping him. The cub stood still while Mark pulled the last of the strangling blackberry streamers from the soft fur. Mark was careful not to touch the animal. He knew that some wild creatures wouldn't accept young that had been handled by humans. He sat and watched the cub in front of him. The Penetrator had his back to the vines. He knew he should move out, but he enjoyed watching this bit of wildlife close up.

The roar came with a built-in crescendo. Mark had never heard anything like it. He knew at once it was the cub's mother. He jumped to his feet, but the she-bear came rushing around the vines, blocking his escape. She was a silver-tipped grizzly, reared on her back legs, roaring maternal fury at this man who was so close to her cub. Mark pulled the .38 pistol, and fired three times in the air. The shaggy, hump-backed grizzly wasn't cowed or frightened by the shots and waddled forward, front claws slashing the air in huge swipes that would break a man's back, or tear his head off his shoulders.

There was no way to escape except by moving backward into the eight-foot-high mass of thorn-filled blackberry vines. If he tried that, he wouldn't get six feet. The she-bear moved closer now, cold red eyes glaring at him. Mark thought of picking up the cub, but that would only make her more furious. Remembering a story from David Red Eagle, Mark jumped up and blasted a mighty roar of his own at the bear. She hesitated, reared higher, curious, staring at him. Mark grabbed the M-16 and dove to the side of the sow over a four-foot-high mass of blackberry vines. He held the M-16 across his chest, hit the ground on his shoulders and back doing a neat forward roll, and came to his feet, running. The rifle hadn't been damaged.

The she-bear made a quick movement toward him, found she was blocked by the irritating vines, then ignored him.

Mark ran twenty yards from the big bruin before he looked over his shoulder. She was licking her cub, nosing it back toward some hidden den from which it had wandered.

Mark scowled at the pair, then trotted another half mile toward the lake, which he could now see through the trees. The stretch of water was large, miles long. He sat on a log and took stock. He had an M-16 and eleven rounds of ammunition, the .38 had been dropped in his scramble to grab the M-16, and the bow and arrow was gone too, back by the blackberry plants. What he needed were a dozen more magazines for the .223.

A night infiltration attack on the lodge area would be best, but Mark didn't want to waste time by waiting for darkness. By the sun's position he guessed it must be about an hour after noon. If he waited until morning another innocent victim might be slaughtered. He had to move now.

Mark estimated his route toward the lodge. He could hit the shoreline and follow it, but that would be the most dangerous. He would strike cross country, come at the place from the back and hope their security wasn't that tight.

As Mark trotted toward the camp, he began to feel the effects of his *Sho-tu-ça* powers wearing off. So he concentrated on the sacred words and phrases as he moved, and soon he felt rejuvenated. The trot was a ground-eating pace that could move him more than forty miles in eight hours and leave him ready to work or fight.

When he came to the gully, he decided he had to follow the forested razor back he was on rather than go down and back up the far slope. He had some distance he could sacrifice to the lakeside, so he moved.

As he worked through the forest he heard the helicopter again, out on a criss-crossing search pattern. Whenever it came anywhere near where he was, Mark simply froze against a big fir and became invisible to the searchers in the chopper. As he trotted along he tried to establish an attack plan. But he couldn't. He hadn't ever seen the lodge. He guessed it would be two stories, perhaps of log construction if it had been there a long time. There would be a staff. Would they be sheep or goats, innocents or hoodlums in this murderous game? No, in this operation there could be no innocents.

He had classified the guards and he knew what he would do with the cages.

Mark found himself being forced more and more toward the lake. A large meadow opened ahead and he resisted the idea of crossing it to save time. There was knee-high grass, not enough to hide in, but if he walked through it, his feet would leave a path that would be easy for the chopper lookouts to spot from the air. He took the next best course and skirted the meadow, staying in the edge of the woods.

The Penetrator had just passed the meadow and moved into the heavy timber again pointing toward the lodge when a green-camouflaged figure forty feet up a second-growth fir at the edge of the meadow pulled out an antenna on his handie-talkie and pushed the send button.

"Lookout four to bird."

"Go, four."

"Have just spotted target moving around meadow from the north, heading toward lodge. He was screened from me so I couldn't get a sure shot."

"Good, four. Dismount and move to point three to show the team in that area the place where he entered the woods again."

As the thin young man climbed down the tree, his bare arms showed dozens of needle tracks. He knew exactly what he was doing, why he was there. When you really need a fix, there is no limit, no line you won't cross for the right connection, one where the junk is there every time.

Mark moved ahead cautiously. He guessed he was about two miles from the lodge. He had taken a side trip to make visual contact with the lake, then continued forward. The Penetrator heard the chopper again, but it was at least a half mile ahead of him. They were still looking.

The Penetrator advanced more slowly now, aware that there might be outposts, lookouts. He had seen nothing so far to alert him, but his instincts told him something could be showing soon, a kind of outer perimeter that Utah surely would have thrown up. Mark wondered how many combat troops the hoodlum had in this outfit, and if they all had 'Nam experience.

A short time later the Penetrator was on a hill slanting down to the lake. It was a half mile slope and he stayed in the middle of it as he worked toward the lodge. He guessed he was still over a mile from the main camp.

The chopper came back, circling, then he saw it settling down ahead of him. Mark ran to where he could see the small clearing. The chopper let out four armed men. All wore the green and black camouflaged battle uniforms. All had long black weapons Mark was sure were M-16s. He saw the men form a skirmish line ten yards apart and start working across the opening and into the woods directly toward him. How did they know where he was?

He studied the situation. Outflank them. He would push deeper into the woods, uphill and simply go around their short line. He was moving then, jogging up the slope, but had gone only a hundred yards when a rifle cracked and a bullet tore through his pants leg, missing the flesh. He hit the dirt and rolled behind a tree.

Mark had heard the report behind him and knew it was the snarl of an M-16. But where was it? He peered from around the base of a tree and looked over the area, then at the trees. The sniper could be behind any one of fifty trees. Mark's eye caught a slight movement and he looked upward. Less than one hundred feet from him in a fir he saw a strange mass of green branches twenty feet off the ground. There was another movement. Cautiously Mark brought up his M-16, laying it on the ground at the base of the tree, flicking it to single shot mode. He waited. The movements came again. Mark aimed at the center of the strange green branches and fired a pattern of three quick shots in a foot-wide triangle.

A long low scream stabbed into the woodsy silence after the sound of the shots trailed off. The moan turned to a sob and slowly the green mass of branches fell, sliding down a limb, then dropping to the ground from ten feet with a thump. It didn't move. Mark could see the man now. He had tied fir branches to himself as camouflage.

The Penetrator could use his ammo. He made a dash for the next tree, but the form on the ground ahead didn't move. Mark knew the skirmishers were coming. He took a calculated risk and ran toward the body, his M-16 on automatic. If the man so much as breathed heavily Mark would riddle him with .223 caliber calling cards. There was no movement.

Mark saw that two of his bullets had taken the man near the center of his chest, probably shattering upward into his heart and lungs. Mark pried the lifeless fingers from the M-16, jerked the magazine from it and found three more full magazines in the man's pack. He had put them in his pockets when he heard the chopper coming again.

This time a bull horn blared at him.

"You might as well give up, whoever you are. We have a team of experienced combat veterans in this area, advancing on you with orders to shoot to kill. There is no way out. Give up now, and we'll spare your life. We just want you off our land."

Mark slid behind another tree out of sight and worked uphill again to outflank the line of skirmishers. He ran low, rifle held just off the ground as he came to denser timber. The fraggers came again, three or four of them and for a moment the explosions seemed to be following him. But they weren't.

157

He paused and looked around a big tree. Something had flashed in his consciousness, something he thought he saw ahead. He wasn't sure what it was: movement or some noise?

Then he saw them, four more men, all camouflaged, and each with an M-16 rifle. The trap was closing.

Chapter 13

RETREAT? . . . HELL!

The Penetrator watched the men move. These were not trained fighting soldiers, they didn't know how to use cover or concealment, they didn't even hold the M-16s like they knew what to do with them. Mark was prone behind a tree as he let them come. The troops behind him were at least six hundred yards away, so he had two or three minutes of free time. The gunmen ahead of him moved cautiously, watching, looking.

Mark waited until they had to cross a small open area in the timber. When they hit the middle of the open space, he would fire. He kept the M-16 on single shot to conserve his ammunition.

Mark picked the farthest man for his first shot. He'd have more time to sight in on him. When the line reached the exact spot he wanted, Mark fired. He didn't even watch the first bullet hit. He was sure it was true. He swung the rifle to the right, sighted in on the second man, who had turned toward the sound of the shot, but had not hit the dirt as any combat veteran would have done with the first firing. Mark snapped off the second round quickly, but when he moved for the third and fourth men, they were gone.

The last two had heard the shots and dove for the ground, where they squirmed behind a log and stayed there. The Penetrator checked the first two targets. One was down and not moving. The second had thrown his weapon away and was trying to crawl behind a tree. Mark came up from his cover and ran ten yards to a large tree, made it with no fire, and quickly moved to the next fir. There had been no movement from the log. Mark made one more short dash and could see behind the cover.

The third and fourth warriors huddled on the ground, their rifles pointing in the direction where Mark had been. Mark killed one with a quick shot, and the fourth man jumped up and zig-zagged away from Mark toward the oncoming line of searchers.

Mark ran for the log, found two full magazines on the dead man, grabbed them and sprinted back into the heavy timber. Then he ran on toward the lodge. He had enough magazines now, and was ready for a real fire fight. But at this point the Penetrator didn't expect a pitched battle. Most of the guards and hunters must have been out after him.

The Penetrator still moved with caution, watching the trees as well as the ground. He came to the edge of the lake and looked toward where he thought the lodge would be. It stood there, lonely, three stories tall, made of both logs and lumber. Half a dozen boats swung on ropes at a dock built into the lake. He went into the forest and began to circle toward the back of the building.

Silently he moved through the forest, using it to his advantage, approaching the back of the big lodge out of the shadows of the heavy woods. Mark watched a guard on the rear door for a full minute before he decided the man wasn't just a scared kid. This one probably had track marks on both arms, and plenty of bullet scars on his body.

Mark leveled the M-16 from his hip, ready to step out into the sunshine and challenge the guard, but he stopped, decided he still needed silence at this point. He faded to the closest point of woods to the lodge, and when the guard looked the other way, Mark ran lightly to the edge of the building, screening himself from the watchman. Then he crept to the corner of the lodge. The guard was looking the other way. Mark thought of using a garrote, but it was too risky—he was too far away. He wished he had Ava, his silent CO-2-powered dart gun, or his thin wrist knife. Mark pulled the bayonet from his belt and balanced it. Then he held the end of the blade with his four fingers and palm. The bayonet was not made for throwing, but he could try. He'd never thrown a bayonet in 'Nam, where he used smaller knives.

It was thirty feet to the rear door where the guard stood. Mark hefted the long knife once more, then running silently forward, he threw the knife. The weapon spun once and slammed into the guard's head, handle first. The man gave a surprised grunt and slumped to one side, bringing up his .38 revolver. Mark kicked his wrist before the guard could fire, spinning the revolver away. The guard was groggy, but still fighting. Mark's big arm clamped around his neck and tightened. Mark hoisted the guard off his feet with a classic "sleeper" hold. His arm cut off the blood flow up one of the carotid arteries to the brain. In fifteen seconds the man passed out. Mark dragged him inside the back door.

He was in a utility room. Quickly the Penetrator tied up and gagged the man, stuffed the guard's .38 in his own belt and silently checked the building. He found no one on the first floor. He moved through the second story, again with negative results. On the top floor he found a two-way radio sender and receiver, which he smashed with the butt of the M-16. In the second room he checked, he found the girl who had been in the cage beside him. She was still naked, spreadeagled on the bed. Mark cut her free, untied her bonds and found a man's shirt and a pair of old pants in one of the dressers in the room for her to put on.

She didn't say a word when he came in, or when he cut her free or gave her the clothes.

Only when she was dressed, did she react, giving a long sigh.

"Then you're not going to rape me too?"

"I told you I'd get you out of this, remember? I was in the cage beside you."

"Oh, yes, you're the one, the maniac. I remember. Now where is that bastard Antonucci?"

"Dead."

"You?"

"Right."

"Good. What about the other bastard, Johnny Utah?"

"He's around, somewhere."

"I want him."

"So do I," Mark said.

"I'll share him with you."

Mark pulled the .38 from his belt, checked the chambers and handed the gun to the girl.

"Thanks . . . thanks for . . . you know."

They left the room and prowled the rest of the house. No one was there, not even a cook.

"They sent everyone out into the woods to find you," she said. "You gave them a fit by winning out there."

"The cage guards?"

"Some of them must still be around. The spares went into the bush."

They ran from the house. Mark had found a bow, and strung it, taking two arrows. He held all three in his right hand as he ran, one arrow nocked, the other tip-upward in the hand holding the bow, the way his ancestors had done a hundred years ago. He had two quick shots with the bow in a few seconds.

At the edge of the woods they paused and peered at the cages. One guard stood outside the shack. Four of the cages were occupied. The guard had a rifle slung over his shoulder.

Mark estimated it was a twenty-yard shot. Easy. He handed the girl his M-16, took the bow and a second later pulled and released. It flew a little high of his heart aim, the wide steel arrowhead point slashed through the right side of the guard's neck, slicing open his trachea, and cutting the right carotid artery. The man grabbed at his throat, his scream stillborn by the severed windpipe. He fell on his side and rolled, trying to get up his M-16 to fire a burst, but the blood supply to the right side of his brain had stopped, and seconds later he passed out. He had bled to death by the time Mark and the girl ran up to him. Mark hurried to the shack, and with the rifle on automatic, kicked open the door and sprayed the interior with .223 caliber hot lead death. No one was inside.

He came back, jammed a new magazine into the M-16 and pulled the girl with him as he ran behind the cages.

"Jesus, what the hell is going on out there?" the man in the end cage asked. He was naked and had bruises on his face and two fresh knife marks on his back.

Mark held up his hand for quiet. He expected some help to surge in if there were any still around the area. Two minutes went by, then someone ran in and screamed when he saw the dead guard. He was a rangy man with hoodlum written all over him. He checked to be sure the man was dead, then swore, pulled a .45 and shot at the man in the second cage. The slug caught harmlessly in one of the four-by-fours. Mark pumped one M-16 round into the guard's head. He fell with a new right ear canal, the small slug shattering as soon as it hit the skull, slicing his brain into a dozen unrelated, non-functioning fragments.

Mark took the girl's hand and pulled her with him again as he ran back into the cover of the heavy timber. They moved twenty yards into the woods and stopped.

"They'll have some kind of reinforcements soon," Mark said. "We have to work out a plan."

"I heard them talking. They had six men left. Utah said they would outfit them like Marines and go hunt you down."

"Six, only six? I can account for three of them. Anyone on the helicopter? Or was that just Johnny and the pilot?"

The girl nodded. "He said just the two of them in the air."

"I thought he had more men than that."

"They did, but you kept killing them." The girl looked up, her pretty face hard now, angry, cruel. "You have to save Utah for me. I want him. I owe him."

Mark thought of the rape, the degradation. He nodded. "If we get him in one chunk, he's all yours, and the rest of the caged people. They have a right to a piece of him."

The girl agreed.

The Penetrator tried to figure out what Utah would do next. His guess was that the hoodlum would find the wounded men, and they would admit the target got away from them and headed for the lodge. But then would Utah come back here, knowing that his enemy had the home ground and all the arms he needed?

Yes, Mark thought, Johnny Utah would have to come back. His nature would not allow him to run away, defeated. He had been a winner all his life. Even if it were by crooked, underhanded and criminal means, he had been a winner. He would be back.

As he decided that, Mark heard the *whupping* of a chopper as it came in from the lake. It landed somewhere near the shore so no one at the lodge could fire at it.

"Will you stay here?" Mark asked the girl.

She grabbed his hand. "No. I want to be sure you don't kill that slob before I get to him. Capture him. Just capture him."

They moved through the woods quietly. They came to the edge of the trees near the main lodge. Two men walked toward the building, with Johnny Utah in front, packing an M-16. Mark settled against a tree and drilled a shot into Utah's right thigh.

"Throw your weapons down; you don't have a chance," Mark bellowed at the pair from thirty yards. Utah had been shoved back by the force of the bullet and fell to his side. The rifle was still in his hands.

"Don't try it, Utah. I'll cut you in half before you get off a single shot."

Utah scowled and dropped the rifle.

"Yeah, yeah, you win. Now get me to a damn doctor before I bleed to death!" It was a demand.

The helicopter pilot agreed.

"Yes, he's right, Mr. Utah is seriously injured. Let me fly him out to a doctor at once. I'm unarmed."

Mark and Marci came out from the underbrush and faced the two men from twenty yards. Kneeling beside Utah, the pilot looked at Mark over his shoulder.

"He's bleeding badly, we'd better hurry." Even as he said it the man pulled up a pistol and fired. Mark's M-16 was at his hip as he saw the gun. He snapped off two shots, then a giant hand slammed into his leg and tumbled him backward. He dropped his rifle and realized that a heavy-caliber bullet had hit his leg.

Mark rolled over and looked at the pilot. He was on his knees, holding his chest, then he toppled and Mark saw the limp, lifeless face and the man's eyes blink open in a death stare.

Marci was beside him then, with the rifle, helping him to stand. At least his leg wasn't broken. Mark hobbled to a spot ten feet from Johnny Utah and looked at the two men. Utah was moaning.

"Check the pilot and see if he's dead," Mark told the girl. "Then take his shirt off."

The girl shook her head. Mark moved over, felt for a pulse, then ripped off the pilot's shirt. Mark tore the cloth into a long strip and a square he could fold. Then he unzipped his pants and pulled them down so he could bandage his wound. The bullet had gone in his leg, but hadn't come out. He saw the .45 lying beside the dead man's hand and frowned. He folded some cloth and pressed it against the wound, then wrapped the bandage around his leg, holding the compress in place to stop the bleeding. His leg hurt like hell, but he knew he could walk on it.

The Penetrator felt the effects of the *Shotu-ça* wearing off and knew he soon would be very tired. He pulled up his pants and zipped them. The girl had been watching him.

"Utah, where the hell are the rest of your men?"

"Men? Rats! They broke and ran when they found out you got past us. Two of them didn't run far, I dropped them with one shot each. The others are hiking out to Vancouver for all I care. You killed the other three."

"Any more hunters, or guards?"

"Hell, no. You killed half of them, you bastard."

The girl still had the .38 as she walked up to him. She raised the weapon slowly.

"Look at me, Johnny. Watch me and remember what you and your animals did to me!" The blast of the .38 sounded harsh, but the bellow and roar of pain from Johnny Utah drowned it out. The slug slammed into his left leg, boring a neat, nonfatal hole.

"Don't worry, Johnny, I'm not going to kill you yet, no way. You got to suffer a lot like we did, like *I did*." She laughed. "Remember when you told me I just had a low pain threshold? We're going to find out just where yours is, me and the other caged animals back there."

Johnny turned to Mark.

"For God's sakes, man, she's going to torture me! You can't stand there and let her do that?"

Mark knelt in front of Johnny Utah and slapped his face, slamming his head to one side.

"I can't? Just watch me, Johnny, watch me!" Mark saw the expression of terror slide over Johnny's face. A scare would be good for the hoodlum. These victims of his deserved at least to watch him die. But there would be no blood orgy, no drawn-out torture. Even though Johnny Utah had turned hundreds of men and women into turkey corpses, Mark couldn't let it happen to him, no matter how foul and terrible Utah's life had been.

Chapter 14

GENTLY FLOWS THE BLOOD

"Stay with him," Mark told the girl, before hobbling back to the cages. She understood what he was going to do and waved.

When Mark got to the pens, he saw the four men at the doors. He let Lew Willet out first.

"What the hell is going on? Where is Johnny Utah? Is everyone dead?" Willet asked.

Mark released them all and told them briefly what had happened and that they were all free. Besides Willet and the man with the two wounds on his back, there was a tall man in his thirties with curly black hair all over his chest. The fourth prisoner was small and thin, with shoulder-length blond hair and soft blue eyes.

"Where is that son of a bitch," the hairy man snarled. "I want to tear his goddamned arms off!"

"Look, first, let's go up to the lodge and find you some clothes," Mark said. "Some of the hunters' stuff should fit you. Then you can deal with Utah."

The men nodded, and Mark took them in

the back door of the lodge and told them to come out at the opposite side. Mark went around to where Utah lay in the dirt by the side door.

Marci had just clawed her fingernails down Johnny Utah's face, leaving three deep bloody scratches.

"Bitch!"

Marci kicked his wounded leg, and Johnny hissed in pain.

"You owe me, Utah. You got me into this mess, and you're going to pay plenty."

Mark came and sat down beside the girl. "The others will be out soon, they're finding some clothes."

"I've got a suitcase in there somewhere."

"We'll get it before we leave."

The men came running out then, two wore only pants, two had on shirts as well. They ringed the downed hoodlum. The man with the slashes in his back kicked Johnny in the side.

"Knife me, will you, you bastard!"

The man with the black hair started for Johnny, but Marci held up her hands, and he stopped.

"Hold it. Just hold it. He owes me the most. I know all of you have a right to a chunk of his hide, but I've got the biggest claim." She paused. "You guys know anything about Johnny Utah? He runs the biggest heroin operation in the country in Detroit. He likes to shoot people who get out of

172

line. Sometimes he doesn't kill them right away, he likes to see them suffer."

"Oh yeah?" the long hair said. "So let's make the prick suffer a little himself."

Lew Willet's mouth had hardened into a firm line. His eyes pinched together and frown lines etched his forehead. "No, we save him for the law. He's a killer, he'll get punished. If you won't do that, count me out. I'm not going to torture a human being, and I won't have anything to do with killing. Not even a sick creep like him."

Marci ran toward him, waving the .38. "Then take a hike, buster!" she screeched. "You don't help, you don't get to watch!"

Willet turned and walked into the lodge without looking back.

Mark stepped up beside Marci, and before she realized it, he stripped the .38 from her hand. "Hold it!" His voice snapped. "This is not a butchering ground or a torture chamber. Willet might be right at that. Johnny Utah is hurting a lot already. I have to go out to make sure the chopper is in one piece and ready to fly, unless all of you want to walk fifty miles to get out of here." He looked at them; they all backed off a little. "Sure, Utah is a killer, a warped, vicious dog of a man who would, and probably has, tortured his own brother. But we don't have to sink as low as he is. Now everybody just take it easy and we'll be back in Twist Lake before dark." He began limping toward the lodge. "Just take it easy on Johnny Utah."

Mark walked away then, taking the guns with him, the two M-16 rifles and both pistols. At the lake front he checked out the chopper. He had flown similar models, and there was room to take everyone on one flight. It even had plenty of fuel, and he had taken the ignition key from the dead pilot on his way. It fit; there should be no trouble. He thought of keeping the M-16s, but then remembering the stringent gun laws of Canada, he decided he better not and threw them both as far as he could into the lake. The authorities would have enough to find when they moved in here.

He checked the ship once more, then hobbled back to the front of the lodge and went inside. He had hoped to find some records, an office setup. Mark found nothing but a safe. He looked over the small desk and at last saw what he wanted. Three unrelated numbers on a desk pad. He tried them on the safe and the first set was the right combination. The small safe was empty.

Mark heard a scream and knew it came from Johnny Utah. He left the lodge and limped back to the spot where he had left the four. They didn't see him coming.

Johnny Utah had been hung by his heels over a tree limb. Now the four clustered around his body, laughing and hooting as they made small slashes in his naked body with sharp knives. His body was one mass of red from a hundred or more cuts.

"So help me I'll make all of you rich—a hundred thousand in cash for each of you!" Johnny Utah screamed.

They laughed at him.

"Sure, as soon as we got you back where you could get that kind of money, you'd have your goons shoot us so full of holes we'd look like that funny kind of cheese," one of the men said.

Mark came up unnoticed, and for just a second the four parted in front of the mangled and bleeding mobster.

Mark lifted the .38 he still carried and pumped three slugs into the tortured mobster's heart.

Marci turned and stared at him in disbelief. Then she sat down in the dirt and looked at Johnny Utah. The men blinked, trying to absorb what had happened. One by one they turned and walked to the lake, stood in the shallow water near shore and washed the blood off their hands and faces.

Marci went to the lake too, took off her makeshift costume and washed her firm young body clean, then walked naked into the house and found her suitcase.

Mark watched them. Now all that was left was to fly the helicopter out. No problem if his leg held up. It hurt like hell now.

A half hour later Mark landed the chopper near the main clearing at Twist Lake. The only one to meet them was Big Jack, who took one look at the ragged group with ill-fitting clothing and ran for his car. He got out of the little town but only after the three men had bombarded his car with rocks.

It was a strange homecoming. They told nothing about what had happened. Marci had not said a word since Utah died. She had sat close to Mark in the chopper. As soon as they landed she had grabbed his arm and refused to let go of him.

They had agreed they would say nothing to anyone about the death lodge or about Johnny Utah. Someone would discover it soon enough. They didn't want to answer any questions, make any explanations or face any charges. They wanted to be far away and out of it.

Mark borrowed a car and took Willet along to bring back his own car. He found it intact, right where he had left it. Mark changed into some of his own clothes then. He took from his money belt twenty-five-hundred dollars and gave each of them five hundred-dollar bills.

"Don't ask where the money comes from," he said. "Don't ask any questions at all."

Lew Willet looked up and started to say something, then shook his head.

Mark paid his bill at the boarding house, gathered up the rest of his belongings and told Mrs. Loomis goodbye.

When he hobbled back to his Bronco,

Marci sat in the front seat. Her suitcase was in the back, and she had changed into a pants suit ready for traveling. Willet leaned against the fender. He stared at Mark a minute.

"Have you ever been hunting?" Mark asked Willet.

"Yeah, deer, a bear once."

"Those wild animals you shot had more right to live than that skunk back there." Mark was talking quietly. No one else could hear him. "Johnny Utah was living on borrowed time. He had killed over a hundred men, probably close to two hundred. He was an animal himself, a predator who should have been wiped out years ago. Now, don't start getting pangs of conscience or have any bad dreams."

Willet sighed, nodded at last and looked up. "I guess you're right. You still won't tell me who you are?"

Mark shrugged, reached in his pocket and took out a blue flint arrowhead and handed it to Lew.

"An arrowhead?" Lew looked at him. "Hey, are you that guy down in the States who ..." He stopped. "Damn, the Penetrator! I've heard a lot about you. No wonder you got out of your cage. I never thought we'd see you again." He grinned. "Well, maybe see your head in a bucket."

Mark shook his hand and got in the car.

"Don't mention this, Willet, to anyone, right?"

"Right, at least not for a few years. Hey, your leg. You need a doctor. Should be one in Williams Lake."

Mark nodded and started the car.

Marci moved over and snuggled next to him, then held his right arm and put her head on his shoulder. She had washed her hair and combed it out and even put on some pale lipstick, but she still hadn't said a word since Utah died.

Mark drove. They found the longhair and the man with the slashes on his back on the road. Mark gave them a ride. The longhair was headed for Bella Coola, and Mark let him out at Tatla Lake. The other one was going to Williams Lake, so they drove him there. He was moving on north.

Mark drove south from Williams Lake on Highway 97 most of the night. His leg hurt more now, but he had to get away from the area. They stopped somewhere in the big timber country for food, then drove again. The girl still had not spoken. Mark realized he didn't even know her name. He found some soft music on the radio and watched another series of shudders surge through his passenger. She hadn't cried yet, and Mark guessed that might be what she needed.

Mark caught her chin and pulled her face back so she had to look at him.

"It's all right. You don't have to worry

about what happened. It's over, it's all right. Believe me, you're young, and pretty. You can make a new life for yourself anywhere. Antonucci's boys will never hunt for you. It's all right."

She leaned back, staring straight ahead. "The men probably wouldn't have tortured him, you know, if I hadn't been so damn insistent, so brutal. I'm not really that way. I've seen some of it, too much, I guess, and it's catching."

Mark took her hands. "Johnny Utah deserved to die. I should have wasted him with the first shot, not put one in his leg. Maybe I wanted to see him suffer too."

She flashed him a quick look that was neither smile nor frown. "I suspected something like that. Are you with some of the other groups, or with the Mafia, or some super government agent? You're different, somehow."

He didn't respond, and she went on.

"They called you Bill, but that's not your name. I knew that." She sighed. "I'm Marci. Maybe I don't want you to know my real name. All that jazz about the gang rape. I mean, it wasn't ... I wasn't what you'd exactly call a virgin. I was a party girl in New York, then this guy said he wanted to keep me, an apartment, clothes, the whole thing. I didn't know who he was at first. It was like being married, or a high class call girl on permanent call. I was pretty stupid."

Mark started the car and pulled back onto the highway.

"Hey, are you all right?"

He felt the fever coming. Knew it was close, and he wouldn't drive far after it really hit. That bullet must have infected already. He had to find a motel. He had to phone somebody, get some help. He had to find a doctor who would dig that slug out of him and not report it.

EPILOGUE

When the Penetrator awakened he was in a small cottage near a lake. The sun slanted in through an open window, and a radio played softly. When his eyes cleared, he saw a beautiful blonde, reading a book in a chair beside his bed. He watched her blue eyes, then moved his hand, and she looked at him, touched his shoulder.

"Well, I guess you're going to make it. I always wonder, no matter what those doctors say. How do you feel?"

Mark blinked, the girl was still there, the lake still outside the window and the sunlight on the carpet. The girl ... yes, the girl from camp, the naked blonde waif huddled in the cage ...

"Feel?" His voice sounded strange. "Feel woozy, what happened after I folded?"

"Sure you want to know?"

"Exactly."

"You called me Joanna several times. I'm sorry you can't marry her. She's a very lucky girl to know you. I can tell you like her a lot."

"My big mouth. But where did you ever find that doctor?"

"Toombs Antonucci was a bastard but he had friends all over. I remembered a phone call he made while we waited in the Vancouver airport. The name doesn't matter. I explained that one of Toombs' men got a stray slug in his hide and we needed a no-talk medic in a rush. He gave me a name. I phoned him and he dug the lead out of your leg. Over your protests, of course."

"I don't remember."

"He shot you full of penicillin, gave me some tablets for you and bandaged you up. He told me to keep you off your feet for at least a week."

"A week?"

"That's what the doctor said."

Mark was feeling tired again. "I just may put you on the payroll."

"That doctor said he'd never seen anybody as exhausted as you were. Said you had used up so many reserves of energy he was surprised the fever didn't hit you quicker."

"*Sho-tu-ça*," Mark said, thinking out loud.

Sending Marci out for some breakfast, Mark made a long distance collect phone call. The professor sounded alert, if a bit impatient. Mark assured him the assignment was finished, and that he was ready to travel back to the Stronghold. He said nothing of his wound. It would have to wait.

"That is most satisfactory, Mark. Yes,

quite good. There has been no news yet about your situation in Canada. I presume you did not notify the local authorities?"

"I didn't. This one is too hairy. I want to be long gone before they tumble to it. I'll fill you in when I get back."

"That is good, Mark, yes, excellent. I've been worried about another small problem we'll do some thinking about. Along the St. Lawrence Seaway there's been a lot of terrorist activity. It's starting to interfere with normal shipping in that vital link of waterway between the U.S. and Canada. From what I can gather it's some kind of a band of separatists there in Canada doing the damage. I'll have more on it within a week."

"OK. I'll call again when I get the plane headed back your way. I've got to go." He hung up quickly and leaned back in the bed as Marci fumbled with the door, then marched in with a large covered tray.

Marci pushed up the pillows for him so he could eat in bed. She sat and watched him. Mark chuckled as he ate, realizing she was fattening him up for the kill—figuratively speaking. She was as much an expert in her line of work as he was, and he kept getting the distinct impression she wanted to prove to him how good she could be ... and that she could be trusted.

When he finished eating, she put the tray on the end table and came and sat down on the bed beside him.

"You look tired; how about a little nap?"

"Sounds good, but we've gotta move out."

"What!" Marci screamed, somewhat pathetically.

"Sorry, dear. This is all very nice, but ... well, I have a date out west. No, nothing romantic. You might call it business. Feel like a plane ride and some sunshine?"

"But, but the doctor said——"

"I know," Mark grunted. "But I've got a specialist who'll really know how to get me fixed up. A few hours, and I guess I'll live after all." The pain was terrific, but he wouldn't show it.

"You're the boss. Let's go."

Grinning, Mark couldn't help but wonder what old Red Eagle and the professor would think about all this when he limped into the Stronghold with a blonde ...